Suntan... Nude...

At least the name of that color brought interesting images to mind. The types of panty hose boggled Nick's mind more than the colors had. *Ultrasheer? Reinforced toe? Barefoot?* Choosing panty hose for his mother was proving to be harder than he'd thought.

Movement in his peripheral vision disrupted his concentration and he looked up. A miracle appeared at the opposite end of the aisle. Another shopper. A female shopper. *She* would know how to choose panty hose. Those long legs would look terrific in them, too, he realized. His half-awake eyes focused for the first time since he'd gotten out of bed. The jolt of hot coffee he'd gulped before he left home was nothing compared to the stimulant she was. His shoulders straightened. His body went on alert. He slowed to a predatory manner.

Dear Reader,

Get ready to meet the world's most eligible bachelors: they're sexy, successful...and best of all, they're all yours!

This month in **Harlequin Romance®** we bring you the second in a great new series, *Bachelor Territory*. These books have two things in common—they're all predominantly written from the hero's point of view, and they all make wonderful reading!

This month's book is *Marriage on His Terms* by Val Daniels. We'll be bringing you one **Bachelor Territory** book every other month by some of the brightest and the best Harlequin Romance authors. Included in the lineup are Emma Richmond, Lucy Gordon, Heather MacAllister and Barbara McMahon.

Happy reading!

The Editors

BACHELOR TERRITORY

*There are two sides to every story...
and now it's his turn!*

P.S. Look out in **Harlequin Presents®** for our "brother" promotion, **MAN** *Talk* starting April with bestselling author Charlotte Lamb.

Marriage on His Terms
Val Daniels

Harlequin Books

TORONTO • NEW YORK • LONDON
AMSTERDAM • PARIS • SYDNEY • HAMBURG
STOCKHOLM • ATHENS • TOKYO • MILAN
MADRID • WARSAW • BUDAPEST • AUCKLAND

ISBN 0-373-03497-0

MARRIAGE ON HIS TERMS

First North American Publication 1998.

Printed in U.S.A.

CHAPTER ONE

THE call from his mother came at two in the afternoon; the anonymous package was delivered late that evening.

The minute the delivery man placed the same-day express packet in Nick Evans's hand, he felt a sinking dread. The feeling didn't go away as he closed the door and stared at the bulky, padded envelope. No message. No identifiable sender's address.

The generic videotape case he found inside only increased the ominous feeling. Nick knew it had something to do with his unknown grandfather's death.

Nick shoved the tape into his VCR.

For the next ten minutes, he watched a montage of his life. In still photos, he saw himself as a baby, wrapped in a blanket and held by a young version of his mother. He was smiling from a grocery store cart when he was about three; playing in the snow at the park when he was six or seven. As he got older, some of the pictures included his mother. Others with him alone were interspersed with ones of her by herself. About the time he reached junior high school, the pictures became like home movies. He saw himself playing football in college; walking across the stage to accept his diploma.

The last pictures couldn't have been taken more

than six, eight months ago. He was getting out of his truck, the Evans Homes logo on the side, at one of his construction sites. He'd only bought the company nine months ago.

A current version of his mother turned to wave toward a friend, then looked happily back toward the camera. A soft breeze rippled her hair as she got into her car.

If this was from his grandfather, the crazy old man had known everything about her. Them, he modified.

And the only element missing from their lives was his father.

Nick hadn't felt such a sharp pain of longing for his father's gentle presence in ages. The intensity of losing him had dulled in the five years since his death. Nick's memories were happy. His father's release from the pain and suffering of his last few months had been a quiet blessing. But to have his father erased from their lives as if he'd never existed brought Nick an intense pang of grief.

The screen flickered twice, went blank, then an old man, Nick assumed it was his grandfather, came on.

Nick rose, intent on sending the old man into the same oblivion. He had no desire to "meet" the man who had willfully pretended his father, a good strong man Nick had greatly admired, didn't exist. He wasn't about to sit through any more...but the question of why someone would send him this tape stayed his hand.

He sank down into his seat.

"I've missed you, Marsha," the old man began, talking to Nick's mother as if she was in the room.

"Can you tell? I guess you knew I would. So you're probably not surprised I've kept in touch."

Hell! Damn! Nick wondered if it was possible to have his face removed. Except for the old man's age, Nick looked just like him. How dare the man before him be responsible for his own thick mane of hair. His grandfather's was stark white, but even colorless, Nick could see the same curve in his widow's peak, the same unmanageable cowlick right behind his ear. He saw both in his own dark hair every morning, every time he looked in the mirror.

How dare this man give him that straight, strong nose, the squared chin and then pretend the man who'd helped give him life didn't exist.

It gave Nick a little pleasure to note that his physique had come from his father, the broad shoulders and narrow hips. And he had his father's eyes. His grandfather's were cold, icy blue, small, beady. *He* had inherited his father's warm, dark ones.

And his father's height. His grandfather was semi-perched semileaning on the edge of a desk. He'd had to stretch for his short legs to reach the floor. Nick had a good five inches on him. And a lot more strength. The man in the picture looked frail.

"—sure you're wondering, my dear Marsha." Somehow, despite the weak, wavery voice, the tone taunted, teased and heckled.

Nick cringed and decided he'd better pay attention.

"…because I always meant for you to have everything, of course. You knew that, even when you married that man. You were willing to give it up at the time. So let's see if you handle things differently than

I did, my dear. Let's see what you do with a second chance to have something after all those years living on the edge of poverty.''

Poverty? Nick's father had provided them a comfortable living. Not extravagant, but no one would have called him less than successful in his support of his family.

The old man chuckled, a feeble replica of Nick's own deep chuckle and Nick decided he'd never laugh again.

"So to get what's left of my estate—everything except what you've already heard my lawyer give away,'' the image explained, "you'll have to rely on Chet. That's you, Nicholas.'' The old man's lip curled on the name. "I hope you're there with my daughter. You *would* have been named Chet—after me, you know—had she married Paul Donovan like she was supposed to. So you'll have to bear with me if I call you Chet. That's how I've always thought of you.''

The old man stared directly at Nick. At least it felt like it. Nick squirmed uncomfortably. He suspected he was supposed to.

His grandfather laughed again. "You'll like Christine, my dear grandson. I do hope you'll be happy.''

Nick wanted to gag.

"Christine is lovely. You'll make a wonderful pair. And we'll have to leave it up to our grandchildren to fulfill our dreams,'' he said softly. "And you, my dear Marsha, will get what you so richly deserve after all these years.''

Chester Celinski actually winked at the camera and

sketched a salute with his ancient, blue veined hand. "Till we meet again in the next world..." The image held for a minute then blinked off. The screen was an empty gray.

What had that been about? Nick had the feeling he should have been listening to every word instead of studying the old bastard. He grabbed the remote from the corner of the end table and hit the Rewind button. The entire production had been less than fifteen minutes. The part where his grandfather had started talking couldn't have lasted but five of it, maybe less. Nick hit the Play button again and listened impatiently to the first couple of sentences.

"The house, all my financial holdings, my share of Celidon is yours, Marsha, if your son is willing to form the permanent partnership you refused. A permanent partnership with Wylie's granddaughter. Christine has agreed to the marriage, of course. Besides being very attractive, she's no fool. She wants Wylie's assets, which you would get should she turn my grandson's marriage proposal down. My assets—everything you will receive—go to her if my grandson refuses."

The old man had chuckled then. Nick felt a chill run through him. He'd been noticing his inherited cowlick here.

"Don't try to fight destiny." He chuckled again, obviously pleased with seeing himself in that role. "My attorneys have pledged that it's airtight, uncontestable—unless, of course, Nicholas is married by the time you hear this." The man's voice sounded confident that he didn't have to worry about the possibility. Resentment flared that the old man knew him so well. "I wouldn't want to break up a happy union."

"Of course, you old fool," Nick talked back to the image. "Your document would never hold up in court if you tried to make it supercede a prior legal agreement." The sale of one of his houses had recently fallen through for exactly that reason.

But where did that put him? He wasn't married. Didn't plan on getting married. And who the heck was Christine? Why would she go along with this?

Because she'd been blackmailed in the same way, he reminded himself. "And she's no fool," Nick repeated his grandfather's words. "So there must be lots and lots at stake."

His grandfather was rich. "Filthy rich," his father had described him long ago. It was one of the few things Nick knew about the man. His mother had said very little about him. It was his father who had answered Nick's random questions.

He glanced at the empty tape case lying open on the table and picked up the packet it had come in. Who sent it? Why the advance notice? Warning, Nick amended. Someone had wanted to warn him about the situation he and his mother were walking into.

He threw the heavy envelope back where it had been. Well, he definitely did not want to marry a woman picked by some strange, old, sadistic man just to satisfy the man's dreams of controlling the people around him.

"...you'll have to rely on Chet. That's you, Nick," the voice droned on.

The phone rang and Nick jumped. He hit the Mute

as he picked up the cordless receiver and the image of his grandfather took on his mother's voice.

"Are you packed?" she asked from the other end of the phone.

"Getting there," he answered, checking his watch. Almost an hour had slipped by since the package had been delivered.

"You have everything taken care of so you can leave with me bright and early in the morning?" She sounded frail, something Nick never imagined his mother could be. It had no doubt been a tough day for her since she'd called him with her news this afternoon.

"I'm almost ready," he assured her. "How you holding up, Mom?"

"I'm numb," she answered.

"No regrets," he urged gently.

"Just wishes," she said.

The tape had rewound. Nick punched the Play button and watched as the muted images started again.

"I've been going over it all, wishing I could have done something differently. I should have tried to heal the rift with my father."

"You did more than once," he said pointedly. "Do you think the old bastard will leave you anything?" he had to ask. How was this going to affect her? Could she lose her birthright twice in a lifetime and not grow bitter with regret?

She couldn't resist being her usual motherly self. "Your language, Nick," she admonished him before she answered his question. "I have no idea." He could picture the slight shrug he was certain she in-

serted. "Maybe my mother's jewelry? I know I'm in-
heriting something because Mr. Vaughn said I needed
to be at the reading of the Will after the funeral. You,
too," she added. "You're supposed to be there, too."

"You told me," he reminded her. "Does it bother
you that your father will probably give what should
have been yours to some stranger?" Despite her ret-
icence about the man she'd lived there with, his
mother had often talked fondly—lovingly—about the
life she'd lived, the house she'd grown up in.

"I made the choice thirty-five years ago. It's a little
late to second-guess it now."

When Nick was young, he'd thought it was some
sort of reverse fairy tale. The princess who'd given
up her kingdom for the handsome prince.

Nick's father had agonized over what Marsha had
given up for him. If he were here—

"I wish I could have done it without hurting Father.
I always thought—" Her voice broke. She was crying, over *him*.

Nick inadequately tried comforting her. But it was
difficult to offer sincere sympathy when the bitterness
he felt toward the old weasel boiled up in his throat
and threatened to choke him.

"It's okay," she reassured him in a whisper. "It's
okay."

It wasn't. Nick could give her everything, make up
for the pain, for all the tough choices she had made,
if he was just willing to—

"But that isn't why I called, Nick." She sniffed
loudly and coughed once, clearing her words of the
thick sadness. "I need a favor. The stores out here

are closed for the night," she continued. "Could you stop somewhere for me on the way to the airport in the morning. One of those twenty-four-hour groceries?"

"Sure. Anything." Anything, he thought guiltily, except marry some woman his grandfather had picked out for him.

His mother explained the favor she needed and suggested she get off the phone so he could finish getting ready.

"Mom, I wish I had a magic wand I could wave and make everything perfect."

She chuckled. "You've never struck me as the fairy godmother type."

He had the magic wand right in his hand, he realized, juggling the videotape that had automatically ejected from the VCR.

"Nick," her usual steady acceptance of reality was back in her voice, "Your best magic is agreeing to go to the funeral with me. I do appreciate it, Nick."

"I wouldn't let you go alone," he assured her and wanted to tell her about the tape.

"I know you'd do anything on earth you could for me. It's a great comfort, Nick. Now you finish packing," she said quickly. The huskiness in her tone said she was afraid she'd cry again. "I'll see you bright and early in the morning. Don't forget my panty hose," she reminded and rang off.

And Nick suddenly knew exactly what his grandfather had intended to accomplish with his bizarre last will and testament. Chester Celinski had hoped to alienate them, to firmly put a wedge between them the way he'd put one between him and his daughter. His legacy. He was passing it on.

If Nick didn't marry Christine, his mother wouldn't regain what she'd lost. Her birthright. And how could she not resent it? *I know you'd do anything on earth you could for me,* she'd just said.

Even as he told himself Marsha Evans would never feel that way, he knew deep down it would affect their relationship.

And if he did something as foolish as marrying the unknown Christine so his mother could inherit, he'd resent her. Either way, the wedge would be there between them, eating away at what had always been a good relationship.

It was a trap and a curse—not a legacy.

Nick stared at the hosiery display and wondered if there was a conspiracy to make him crazy. His lack of sleep and the impossible choice in front of him made his eyes blur and his stomach knot. The man at the one open checkout stand at the front of the grocery store wouldn't be much help in choosing hosiery, Nick suspected.

Suntan. Mist. Tawny beige. Nude…at least the name of that color brought interesting images to mind. White. There were three variations of beige, he realized with growing dismay.

He should have asked more questions. But he'd had other things—more important things—on his mind and his mother's request had sounded so simple.

The sizes boggled his mind more than the colors had. He grabbed two egg-shaped packets from the rack and compared the print on the packaging. Ultra sheer? Reinforced-toe? Barefoot?

Movement in his peripheral vision disrupted his concentration and he looked up. A miracle appeared at the opposite end of the aisle. Another shopper. A female shopper. The woman stopped and frowned at the shelves in front of her.

She would know how to choose panty hose, Nick thought with relief and headed for her purposefully. Those long legs would look terrific in them, too, he realized. His half-awake eyes focused for the first time since he'd gotten out of bed. The jolt of hot coffee he'd gulped before he left home was nothing compared to the stimulant she was.

His shoulders straightened. His body went on alert. He slowed to a predatory saunter.

He was almost within speaking distance when she glanced his way. With a bug-off-weirdo warning in her eye, she pulled a bag of dog food from the shelf. Without another acknowledgment of his existence, she started back toward the front of the store.

"Wait."

She didn't even hesitate. The appealing sway of her hips beneath her worn and faded jeans distracted him until he reminded himself of his desperate situation. "Wait! Could you help me?" he called, almost catching up with her.

Her over-the-shoulder "No," caught him off guard.

"Please?" He hated to beg.

She finally stopped in view and shouting distance of the male clerk at the front of the store. The light dawned. At four o'clock in the morning, no sane woman accepted overtures from a stranger in an all-night grocery store—even one dressed in his best and only suit.

She was easy to look at *and* had brains. She was being cautious.

"Look, I..." How did you ask a knockout, drop-dead gorgeous woman to help you pick out panty hose? He frowned his distaste and she looked ready to stalk away again. Her eyes narrowed suspiciously. Did *he* look that disreputable?

"Would you help me pick a pair of panty hose for my mother?" he blurted.

Those big green eyes widened. A smidge of amusement hovered just beneath the emerald surface.

"Look. When my mother asked me, I thought it would be as simple as grabbing a package." He had to brace himself to keep from shuddering. "One look at that display back there, and I realized I'm in way over my head." He added a helpless twist to his smile and hoped he looked like a lost little boy. The look had always worked to get his papers typed in college.

She shifted the ten-pound bag of dog food and glanced toward the kid at the cash register again. "Okay," she finally agreed.

Nick moved a step closer and her wary look returned. "Let me take that," he explained his movement as he took the dog food from her arms.

Without another word, she sidestepped him and started back the way they'd come. "What's your mother wearing for whatever she needs these for?" she asked skeptically over her shoulder.

Nick had to lengthen his steps to keep up with her.

"I have no idea," he said irritably as she stopped in exactly the place he'd been standing a minute before.

"What kind of clothes does she usually wear? What colors," she added when he didn't answer right away. "Pastels? Bright colors?"

"She wears a lot of black and white. She'll probably wear black," he added, remembering why she needed the hose.

"What size?"

"If I knew that..."

"I mean how big is she? Petite? Taller than you..." Her grin was friendly, encouraging, and he realized she finally had noticed something about him. She obviously approved of his height.

"She's about your height and build, maybe a little...thinner."

The woman straightened. The smile was gone. Nick fought the urge to defend himself. He couldn't exactly tell her his mother wasn't as generously proportioned in certain areas of her anatomy, especially since that particular area had nothing to do with panty hose. He mentioned the size that had stayed in his mind. "Maybe queen-size?"

Her disdain turned to irritation. She tapped a long, graceful finger against a height and weight chart posted at the side of type display. He hadn't noticed it before. "She's *smaller* than I am?"

He studied the weights on the chart and realized his mistake. Damn. Why were women so sensitive over their weight? "I thought...she's very queenly. Regal. I thought..." He shrugged. He obviously wasn't getting out of this one gracefully. "It sounded right," he murmured.

"You should be safe with either of these colors." The woman lifted her head regally, stuffed two packages of panty hose at his chest and took her dog food out of his arms.

"But which?"

"I suggest you buy both. You'll be safe that way." She stalked away before he could say anything else.

"Hey thanks," he called.

"No problem," she returned without looking back.

He stood mesmerized, staring after her, watching the long legs stride away. The sway of her hips set her hair swinging the opposite way in counterpoint. The light brown color caught the store's bright lights in its strands, turning it blond. Or tawny beige, he thought. Maybe *that* was tawny beige.

With a sigh and a look at his watch—he'd lost twenty minutes. He expected this to take five—Nick came out of his daze. If he fiddled around much longer, he was going to miss the flight.

The college-aged male cashier gave Nick the look he'd expected from the girl he'd asked to help him. "For my mother," he explained self-consciously and the kid looked as if he wanted to say, "Hey, it isn't my business who you buy panty hose for."

The girl, who had finished paying for her dog food as Nick approached the checkout, walked past the front windows.

"Not very busy this time of day," Nick commented.

The young man gave him his change.

"Not on weeknights," the cashier confirmed, slanting a look at the clock over the exit behind him. "Things'll pick up in another hour or so."

Nick started to pocket his change, heard an abbreviated scream and froze.

The cashier rose to his tiptoes as they both stared toward the window. Every nerve ending in Nick's body screeched as he took in the slow-motion scene outside.

The foxy lady who'd helped him pick the hosiery was standing beside a white car, her keys in one hand, the other in the air as if she hoped to flag a taxi. Her face matched the color of her car. Her mouth hung open.

Two feet from her, and moving away fast, a gangly, scruffy-looking man swung a purse—her purse, Nick realized—to his chest. He cradled it like a football and increased the length and pace of his stride with every step.

Nick took off at a sprint. He swore as he waited for the automatic door to slide open far enough to squeeze through. That delay cost him a good ten feet on the thief.

The thin man was halfway across the empty parking lot when Nick finally hit the cool morning air. His breath puffed out before him as he gave chase. Damn. Dress shoes weren't made for running, and though the suit wasn't as heavy as the protective pads he'd worn playing football, it was confining.

For a moment, that's where he was. The adrenaline pumped as frantically as it had in the conference championship when his team had been up by three and he'd been the one thing between the goal line and the determined punt receiver. And the time was ticking out.

The purse snatcher tripped over a concrete parking stop, wobbled and regained his balance after stumbling a couple of steps. He veered right, toward the back of the store.

Nick turned up his speed, rounded the corner of the building where the purse snatcher had disappeared and realized he'd gained several yards on the scum.

He could almost hear a crowded stadium cheer as he closed another three feet. The uproar reached a fever pitch as the running man would have ducked into the dark alley behind the store. Not that this side of the building was light, Nick realized belatedly. Cussing himself for stupidity, Nick prayed the idiot didn't have a gun or knife or something.

All those years of playing Safety on various football teams didn't go to waste. Nick launched himself in a flying tackle at the purse snatcher.

The tackle caught the man's knees. His startled yelp sounded like an abused pup's. He stumbled but somehow managed to stay on his feet. He struggled to kick Nick away.

The thief's shoe connected with Nick's shoulder and he felt his hold slipping. He only had the jerk by one ankle now.

"Dammit." The man's loose foot caught the side of Nick's head and glanced off. "You son of a..." The expletive was cut short as the man danced his way out of Nick's grasp and escaped.

The flat slapping sound of the man's tennis shoes

fled down the dark alley and quickly faded into the quiet predawn.

"Dammit." Nick relaxed his full length momentarily against the asphalt and pounded a fist on the pavement beside him. Lifting himself into a push-up, he got to his feet. Bracing against the smelly Dumpster beside him with one hand, he used the other to dust off his jacket and smooth grit from his trousers.

"So much for playing Superman." He should have known better. He felt a tear in the fabric of his one and only suit jacket. He wouldn't mind the suit as much if his ego was intact. The gorgeous woman was not going to be impressed with a man who bought panty hose and failed at playing hero.

The panty hose! He was going to miss his flight.

As he turned toward the front of the store, his foot caught something solid and sent it skidding. He squinted and reached down to see what he'd kicked. His mouth spread into a wide grin. The purse. The bum must have dropped it when Nick tackled him.

He let the long strip of leather that served as a handle drag against the ground beside him as he strutted back to the front of the store.

She was standing just out of the shadow as he rounded the corner. "Got it," he held the purse proudly to the light.

"Oh, good grief, are you all right?" Her voice shook, her tone was husky, a wisp of sound. The dry sarcasm was gone. Her hand flattened against the rise of her breasts. The second she eased the pressure, he could see her hand tremble.

"Been better." He grimaced. "Didn't catch the bas—"

"Do you think I care? Do you know how terrified I was? I...you..." She shook her head. Her tone turned indignant. "Nothing was worth risking..." She paled even more in the yellowish light. Her skin looked translucent.

Nick draped his arm around her shoulders and pulled her against him. She felt warm, soft, much more fragile than she looked.

"Hey, I got it." He exhibited the purse again, hoping to make her feel better so he could quit feeling inadequate. "No damage done."

"Thank you." She managed a weak smile. "There isn't a thing in here that isn't replaceable," she lectured him in a shaky voice as he pushed it into her hand. "That was crazy." Still trembling, she backed out of his embrace.

"But it sure would be a hassle to replace it all, wouldn't it?" he said, stung by her disparaging tone.

"It isn't funny." She sniffed indignantly. "You could have been hurt. Killed. Do you think this—" she waved the purse in his face "—is worth that?"

He tried to lead her toward the two cars parked in the lot.

She semifollowed, continuing her tirade about the chance he had taken.

Dammit, he should have let her get her own purse. He'd risked his life, not to mention taking a chance on missing his—

His mother was going to kill him.

"You're gonna be all right." He interrupted her

ranting. A solitary car passed on the usually busy street. "You should go in and call the police," he added with a nod toward the store.

She shook her head. "He's gone. It would be little more than a nuisance call."

"But they *should* know some creep is hanging around here in the middle of the night, waiting for unsuspecting victims."

"I'll call them in the morning," she promised. "And I'll let the store manager know."

It was his turn to nod. "That'll work."

She glanced up at him, her eyes still wide and slightly shell-shocked. Her arms were wrapped tightly around her midsection and he had an incredible urge to cocoon her in his own arms to reassure her. But unless he wanted another lecture, he shouldn't waste his time.

As if she knew what he was thinking, she caught her lower lip between her straight white teeth. "I'm sorry. I shouldn't have gone off at you that way. It just scared me." She giggled nervously, then shuddered. "And I do appreciate you risking—"

"I'm risking a lot more now." He couldn't help but smile but he was moving before he finished the sentence. "I'm supposed to catch a flight and if I miss it, I guarantee you, my mom is going to do me serious harm. Much worse than that guy would have." He started for his car. He dug for his car keys and muttered an expletive when his hand came up empty.

"What? What's the matter?" This time, she came toward him, her face filled with concern.

He wished he had the time to enjoy her approach.

"Damn, I tore my pocket. My keys are gone. Look," he moved her aside, "I hate to be rude, but I've gotta call a taxi." He jogged toward the store. Besides, he'd left his mother's panty hose at the checkout stand. He wasn't certain which would be worse: forgetting them or not showing at all.

"You're just going to leave your keys?"

"Don't have time to worry about it," he called over his shoulder. "As it is, I'm going to be running through the airp…"

She caught his arm. "Get in my car." She swung her purse up and hooked it over her shoulder. "Surely you'll let me drive you to the airport after what you just did for me." It was her turn to glance at her watch. "What time's your flight?"

"Five-forty."

"Whew. Fifty-five minutes and we're forty minutes away? A cab would never get here in time, let alone get you there." She held up her hand and dangled her keys. "At least he waited to rob me until after I'd already dug my keys from the bottom of my purse. That'll save us two minutes right there."

He grinned, delighted with the offer and even halfway hopeful they'd make it in time. Solving his problem seemed to be helping her leave the frightening experience behind.

And she was right. Transportation to the airport was a fair trade for the hassle he'd saved her.

"Okay," he gladly accepted her offer.

She crawled into her car and reached for the passenger side handle to unlock the door. He started to get in then remembered. "The panty hose."

She smiled. "Mustn't forget those."

With a be-right-back gesture, he hurried into the store.

CHAPTER TWO

THE cashier was standing by the window, watching the whole drama without lifting a finger to help. "Did you get him?"

Nick grabbed the small paper bag from the counter where he'd left it. "No, but I got her purse. And lost my car keys," he added with a wince. "Look, could you keep an eye out for them? Leave some kind of message with lost and found so someone will know whose keys they are if someone happens to turn them in?"

"Sure," the kid promised. He hadn't moved a muscle and Nick wondered if the kid's assurance was worth much. Not a lot, he figured. But surely nothing too terrible would happen to his car, sitting in a grocery store parking lot.

He hurried out to where the tawny-haired beauty was sitting with her little economy car idling. He folded himself into the passenger seat and gingerly shuffled his feet into the tiny spot on the floor she'd obviously cleared. "You can move more of that if it's in your way." She indicated the books and paperwork with a smile. The back seat was piled even higher. It looked like she lived in the thing.

He wished he was driving, knew with a glance at his watch that he was going to miss his flight.

"I'll get you there," she promised, reading his

mind. "Do you have bags or something?" As soon as she said it, she frowned and brushed the question away. "Oh, no. I hope there's nothing you need out of your car."

He groaned then shrugged. "Guess it doesn't matter."

"How 'bout your ticket? You have it?"

He patted the inside pocket of his jacket, nodding his relief that the little packet the travel agent had sent by courier was still there. Then he checked his back pocket for his wallet. "I'm fine. I'll manage," he told her and himself at the same time. Shoot. There were stores in St. Louis, weren't there? Plenty of them. He'd do some shopping this afternoon. It might be just the thing to help keep his mother occupied.

The woman pulled out of the parking lot and drove like a bat out of hell.

Dawn was peeking over the horizon, turning the dark sky a peachy pink at the edges as she pulled onto the Interstate highway a few minutes later.

"Where you going?" she asked.

"St. Louis." He decided to fasten his seat belt.

"Business?" She glanced at him and he resisted the impulse to suggest she watch the road. At least they still had it mostly to themselves. "I'm sorry about your suit," she added. "Is that going to be a problem?"

He examined the damage. "I probably need a new suit anyway," he decided to make the best of it. The pants pocket seemed to have taken the major brunt of his tussle with the ground. An L-shaped tear had almost turned it inside out. He squirmed under the seat belt to stuff it back in and straightened his jacket. It would cover the tear.

"You'll be okay looking like that when you arrive?"

"I'll have time to buy another one before it's really important."

"You don't have meetings the minute you step off the plane then?" she half commented, half asked.

"I'm not going on business," he answered her earlier question, examining the half inch tear just below and to one side of his knee. He guessed he could live with it. There wasn't a whole lot of choice at this point. He smoothed it. "I knew I shouldn't have put this on today," he muttered to himself.

"Most men avoid wearing suits until they have to," she said a bit smugly.

Intentionally or unintentionally, she kept taking potshots at his ego. Not only was she ready to classify him with "most men," the only thing she seemed to have approved of him so far was his height. Which was probably natural considering she was fairly tall herself. "I don't know what to expect," he explained the suit. "I'm going to help my mother take care of some things," he added, "I didn't want her to have to worry about my appearance."

She smiled. "You're a good son." Ah! That brought approval. Her grin was filled with it. "Hey. Reach behind you. There's a square plastic basket— like a tiny laundry basket—with a tape dispenser," she said. "Get it."

He frowned at her.

"We can tape that."

When he continued to frown, she reached over with one long finger and tapped his knee.

"Make that tear almost unnoticeable. Close anyway."

Jiminy. Did she know what she was doing to him? He subtly squirmed away from her touch. "It's not that big a de—"

"Are you going to have time to buy a new suit before you see your mother?"

"She's meeting me at the airport for our flight, but—"

"The trip must be fairly important or you wouldn't be out at this time of morning—" She said it like she thought getting up this time of day might be a crime. "Rushing around to catch a plane. In a suit," she added.

"My grandfather's funeral," he told her.

Her big eyes widened as she gazed at his face. A look of distress settled on hers. "Oh. I'm sorry." She actually got misty-eyed.

Her empathy touched something in him until he realized she might not be able to see to drive. "No big deal," he reassured her.

If anything, her horror grew.

He wanted to ask her to just watch the road. "He...I didn't know him. I've never met him." He didn't express his low opinion of the man, uncertain whether that would upset her further or calm her down. He was scared to look at the speedometer to see how fast she was going. "He disowned my mother long before I was born. I wouldn't be going at all if I didn't think Mom might need the emotional support. It's going to be tough for her. I didn't want her to be alone.''

Her sad eyes checked the road again. ''Why did your grandfather do something like that?''

''Disown my mother?''

She nodded.

'''Cause she married my father,'' he said dryly.

Her brows rose as she glanced at him.

''I have a little trouble grieving for someone who would have been happier if my father and I had never existed.''

''Then at least we can have you presentable for your mother's sake.'' She shook her head as if it was all still inconceivable and ordered, ''Get the tape.''

He reached around and immediately put his hand on the basket she'd told him would be there. In a surprisingly short time, his hand closed on what had to be a tape dispenser.

''Now, exactly how is this going to work,'' he asked.

''Just roll up your pants leg to where the tear is,'' she said, then whistled appreciatively when he did. ''Nice legs.'' Her impish grin matched the sparkle in her eyes as he glanced at her. He smiled back and wished he'd met her when things were less complicated. He sure wouldn't mind having the time to—

She distracted him from his thoughts by giving him detailed instructions. It took him three tries to get the slight tear in the cloth patched to her satisfaction. ''Almost unnoticeable,'' she finally declared, running her hand across the fabric covering his knee as he rolled his pants leg down. He held his breath as electricity shot through him and other parts of his body clamored for the same attention.

She turned it to his jacket and the hanging string of fabric with a button dangling at the end.

"Tape won't do that one," she said, scowling. She leaned up against the steering wheel and pressed the piece of material back in place with one elegant hand, smoothing it against his chest.

Nick prayed she didn't notice what she was doing to him and straightened his jacket again.

He released his breath when she turned her attention back to the curve she was treating like the Indianapolis Speedway. Shoot, how could she terrify him and turn him on all at the same time. She seemed to be mastering both tasks without trying.

"Try the stapler," she suggested as the road straightened out again. "If you use the little bitty one," she added, "surely we can hide a staple under the button. It won't look great but it will look better than that big rip with cloth hanging."

"It isn't that..." His voice trailed at her distressed I-was-only-trying-to-help look. "...big. Where's the stapler?"

"In the basket. The little one." She corrected him when he pulled out the stapler he'd found. "It's probably in the bottom," she said. "You'll have to dig."

"What do you do? Live in this car?" he asked as he fixed the button to her satisfaction.

She grinned. "No."

"Why do I get the feeling I could find about anything I need in here?" He let himself really look at some of the junk piled in the back seat.

"Probably because you could." She looked smug. "It's my office. We're almost there. I think we're going to make it if you're a good sprinter."

He checked his watch and saw he had almost fifteen minutes before his flight was supposed to leave.

"Be glad this is KCI instead of one of those other airports. You'd never make it if this airport wasn't so nicely laid out."

He tried to get a word in edgewise. Damn. Two more minutes, maybe less the way she drove, and he wouldn't have time to ask any of the questions he was suddenly dying to know answers to.

"Which terminal?"

He told her and hurried to get in a question. "What do you do?" He indicated her "office."

"I run a little everything service." She reached for the dash and plucked a business card from a little clip she had there.

"H.E.L.P. Services—Honest Experts for Little Problems," she quoted as she slipped it into his breast pocket.

"So you do…?"

"Everything," she said almost before he got the "do" out of his mouth. A vision of what he'd *like* her to do clouded his mind. "Within reason," she added, annihilating the image before it could fully form.

"What are you 'doing' at five-thirty in the morning," he asked as she screeched into the appropriate terminal circle.

"Getting ready to go to bed. At least I was," she

added with a broad grin. "After everything that's happened, who knows if I'll be able to sleep."

"I mean job. What kind of job were you doing?"

"Cleaning up after a twenty-fifth wedding anniversary celebration I was hired to organize." She unconsciously batted her eyes at him. Slamming to a halt outside his airline's check-in gate, she leaned into the steering wheel, draped her arms over it and looked at him happily. "You should make it."

He felt reluctant to leave. A glimpse of the clock on her dash said he didn't have a choice. "You're okay?"

Her wide smile tugged at his senses. He felt an impulse to lean across and kiss her. Wasn't that the thing to do when someone brought you to the airport? You didn't just get out and walk away.

"I'm okay," she assured him. "Thanks to you. Now you'd better get."

He opened the door and stepped out into the cool morning air.

"Don't worry," she said quickly. "I'll take care of everything here. Now go. I'd hate to think that mad trip was wasted."

Still, he hesitated. "Thanks." He was forgetting something. "Thank you so much. I really appreciate it."

"Hey, I owe you," she assured him.

"We're even," he said.

"Not even close." She interrupted him. "I didn't risk my life. All I did was help you choose panty hose for your mom."

He thought of her driving and wanted to disagree. She'd risked them both.

"Oh." She called him back as he would have closed the door. "I don't know your name."

"Nick." He smiled. It seemed strange. He felt like he'd known her forever. "Nick Evans."

"You're in the book?"

The phone book, he realized she meant. "Yeah."

"I owe you. Big time, Nick Evans. I won't forget. Now go," she said. "You have thirteen minutes."

He was almost to the door of the terminal when what she had said sank in. She owed him big time. Suddenly, one solution to the inheritance problem didn't seem as far-fetched as it had when he'd considered and discarded it in the wee hours of this morning. "Wait," he called as she pulled away from the curb. "Wait." He ran waving into the almost barren drop-off zone.

She must have been watching in the rearview mirror. Her brake lights came on instantly and she guided the car back to the curb. He hurried to her window. "You don't have time—"

"I know. Wait for me," he pleaded. "I'm not leaving. I don't have time to explain." He held up a hand. "I have to go tell my mother I'm not coming with her—I'll join her tomorrow," he promised as he saw a protest spring to those interesting lips. "Just wait," he begged. "I'll be there for her tomorrow," he assured her.

She finally nodded.

"Wait right here." He pointed at the ground on which he stood.

She nodded again.

"I'll be right back."

He ran to the terminal. He had ten minutes to find his mother, break his news and get her on the plane without him. It would certainly be less complicated if she hadn't boarded. He mentally crossed his fingers and stopped in front of a video screen to check departure gates.

As he started to look up, he saw his mother outside one of the gates thirty feet away, looking pale and anxious.

She breathlessly called a relieved greeting.

"Mom," he called back, stopping her as she turned toward the security gate and started to put her purse on the X-ray belt.

"I thought for sure you'd miss the flight."

"Long story. And I'm not going to come with you right now," he added. He pointedly glanced at his watch. "Look, we don't have time for explanations. Trust me on this, okay?"

She frowned and her sudden attention on his suit gave him just the excuse he needed to get her on the plane without going into detail. "I had an accident this morning," he said. "I'm all right," he added quickly at her look of dismay. "But I don't have luggage, anything. I'm going to have to catch a later flight. Probably not until tomorrow." He gave her a quick kiss. "Once you get there and settled, leave a number where I can reach you on my answering machine. I'll call tonight."

She looked overwhelmed. He gently pushed her toward the gate as the "last call" came over the loudspeakers. "That's you. Oh, wait." She stopped as he waved the small paper sack. "Your panty hose." The security guard smirked as he put the package on the belt beside her purse. With another quick kiss, he nudged his mom through the electronic gate. She hesitantly started for the walkway at the other end of the holding area, her eyes still on him. The look of concern, layered with a simple trust in him, gave him the reassurance he needed to know his "wild idea" was exactly what he needed to do.

"I'll see you tomorrow." He mouthed the words. "Promise." He breathed a sigh of relief when she disappeared through door with the attendant right on her heels.

Nick slowly turned to go back outside to where...

He patted the jacket pocket where she'd stashed her card and pulled it out.

The stylish burgundy print against the clean white background had her flair, he decided. The first two lines said exactly what she'd already told him.

Honest Experts for Little Problems. He smiled. He had *big* problems. But she'd said she owed him—Big Time. He certainly needed her H.E.L.P.! He finally checked his wife-to-be's name. Shelby. Shelby Wright.

He went back outside to where she waited in her car.

With Shelby Wright's H.E.L.P., he could earn back the Princess's kingdom and beat his crotchety old grandfather at his own game.

He smiled. He'd always liked happy endings.

*   *   *

Shelby was still scowling when he settled back in the passenger seat of her car and leaned wearily against his seat. He shifted one long leg and tried moving his seat back another notch.

"I've had as much adventure in two hours this morning," he said as she continued to stare at him, "as I usually get in a year."

"You're not going to your grandfather's funeral?"

"I'm going. But not until tomorrow," he added. "I have something rather important to do today. More adventure," he added wryly.

"What kind of adventure?"

Damn. He liked her smile. It was just a shade impish and a large part of what had made him believe he just might get her to go along with his idea. But now that the idea had formed, he didn't know where to start. He wished he'd considered the "impossible" a little more seriously last night. At least he would have had time to work out some of the details.

"Shelby?" He tested her name and liked it. It was soft, and warm, like the fresh, homemade chocolate pudding his supervisor's wife made for him from time to time. It felt smooth and rich rolling around his tongue.

"Yes, Nick." He liked the way she said his.

"I need to hire you for something. Several somethings, actually."

"You need me to do something for you already?" Her husky laugh warmed him. She waited expectantly.

"First, I suppose we could leave the airport. Can

you take me home? This will be much easier to explain if I can show you something first."

Her eyebrows lifted. "I hope it's something I want to see," she replied with a sassy grin.

He flirted back and held up both hands. "No etchings," he promised and wondered where the sudden awareness between them had come from. Up until now, he'd barely had time to notice, let alone think about, how attracted he was to her. This whole adventure might have a side benefit or two, he decided and found the thought left him short of breath.

"Okay. I'll play along. You wouldn't be stuck here without a car if it wasn't for me. Taking you home is the least I can do."

It's the least I'm going to ask of you. She put the car in gear and zipped out of the airport. He refastened his seat belt.

Before she could ask the questions that flashed in her eyes, he withdrew her card from his pocket and tapped his finger against it. "Exactly what is it that you do?"

"You name it." She tossed her head. "Somehow, I don't think a detailed explanation of my business is why you changed your plans." She looked at him as they exited from the terminal onto the main road. He braced his hand against the dashboard and checked the flow of traffic. Thankfully, it was light—not too surprising this early in the morning—and not a single car had to dodge not to hit them.

"I don't want to offer you a job that would be totally inappropriate," he explained.

"That's the beauty of this business," she responded. "I never know what I'll do—what is totally appropriate or inappropriate—until I hear it. It's never boring," she added. "That's really why I started this. I like variety and challenges."

He liked her, he realized. She was exactly the type he needed for what he was about to ask. God or Fate or someone had been watching over him this morning when she'd entered the grocery store. "So you do absolutely everything."

"Within reason," she warned with another smile. It brightened the day like the sun was starting to brighten the sky. A light flush accompanied the words and suggested she'd picked up on their mutual attraction, too. She lifted her hair off her shoulder in a flustered gesture.

"Within reason," he repeated and hoped his reasons were reasonable enough for her to consider.

"When I started," Shelby continued when he didn't say anything else, "I intended to turn down any jobs I didn't think I could do. The very first request I declined, the woman begged me to at least try to find someone who *could* do what I said I couldn't." She lifted one shoulder. "So now, besides 'doing' things, I 'find' people to do them and get paid for that, too. It's like a game, and I haven't turned down a job in a long, long time."

Nick knew his grin broadened. He couldn't stop it. So she wanted a challenge?

Curiosity brimmed from Shelby's eyes as she gazed at him again.

He enjoyed watching her frown deepen. He enjoyed watching her, period, he admitted. And she was going to turn him down flat once she knew what he wanted, he thought. The idea of "hiring" a wife had descended out of the blue and it was a crazy one. But he wasn't sure why he hadn't thought of it sooner. If he had to get married, a wife he hired couldn't expect much from him. The man who paid the piper called the tune, didn't he?

I'm offering her a job. Just another little problem for an honest expert. The worst she could do was turn the job down.

"Is it something to do with your grandfather's funeral," she asked with sudden concern.

"Sort of," he said dryly. *Understatement. What an understatement.*

"But could you go with your mom? Is it something I could do without you actu—"

"Believe me, she'd be glad I stayed to take care of this if she knew anything about this in the first place." He took a deep breath and they were mostly silent the rest of the way as Shelby followed his directions to his home.

He'd thought she was pretty earlier, but daylight made her dazzling. A gentle breeze lifted a strand of the brownish, blond hair from her shoulder as she got out of the car. She caught the strand before it could flutter over her eyes, pushed it against her long neck and held it there. Nick watched as her long, exquisitely proportioned body flowed toward him, her whole face glowing with a smile.

It struck him that for all he knew, she might already be married. Or involved with someone. But he'd swear she wasn't attached.

Alarm bells went off in his mind. There were dangers he hadn't thought of in this situation.

"Nick? Is something wrong?"

Nick shook his head and willed his sudden bout with nerves to calm. "Hopefully you're going to make it all right." Her frown urged him to continue. "It all depends on you."

He put his hand to the back of her waist and guided her toward the house then stopped abruptly when he remembered his keys. They couldn't get in. How could he show her the tape?

"I don't have my keys," he muttered, adding a curse under his breath.

"So we need to go to the store and find your keys," she said, automatically starting back for the car. "Or use the keyless entry." She pointed at the small computerized pad hanging beside the garage door.

Of course. How could he have forgotten? The gadgets were a standard feature on all his houses now. A great selling point, several Realtors had told him. He felt like a fool that she'd had to notice and point it out. He had a feeling she noticed everything.

"I've only lived here a couple of weeks," he explained, hoping he could remember the combination. "I've never used it," he added and lucked out on his first try. The door rumbled up on its tracks.

"You live here with..." She let the rest of the question ask itself.

"Just me," he said, extending his hand as he stepped aside and invited her to precede him.

"Big house for a single man," she said as she passed him.

"I plan to change that soon," he couldn't resist rewarding her fishing expedition.

"Lucky girl," she said, giving away absolutely nothing as he lightly grasped her arm and coaxed her into the house.

"I'm glad you think so." Her skin felt like satin under his fingertips. A soft hint of her perfume enveloped him as they moved. "I hope you don't have other commitments today. If you agree to…do what I'm going to ask you to, I'm going to need your help for the rest of it."

"I knew I'd be out late with that party last night. I didn't schedule anything for today." The last couple of words were almost smothered beneath a yawn. "But I hope it isn't something I need active brain cells for or you're in trouble."

"Most people don't use many brain cells when they do it," he said wryly. At least she had *time* to marry him. He didn't have to ask her to cancel other appointments. "It'll probably extend another couple of days," he added, realizing how complicated this could become.

"I don't generally schedule things on the weekend." She confirmed she had the time he needed while at the same time cautioning him that she wasn't making a firm commitment until she knew exactly what he was asking.

"Would you have an objection to going with me to St. Louis?"

"To your grandfather's funeral?" She scowled.

All he really needed was a piece of paper. Her signature on a marriage license and a few words in front

of a justice of the peace would make him more than
happy. A few additional days would probably make
the whole thing a breeze. Who'd ask questions if he
came to the funeral with a bride on his arm? "It
wouldn't be crucial for you to go, but it would make
things easier," he said, then promised, "You'll understand in a minute."

She grimaced skeptically. "Maybe it's time I see
whatever it is you plan to show me."

"Past time," he agreed.

CHAPTER THREE

THE videotape lay in the middle of the kitchen counter where he'd tossed it before he'd walked out the door early this morning. It already seemed like a lifetime ago. He'd decided not to take it with him. Proving he knew about his grandfather's "ultimatum" wouldn't help his mother at all. At the time, he'd thought nothing would, except marrying a stranger named Christine.

He'd considered that seriously. Nothing in the old coot's tape said they had to live together or even act like they knew each other. And since he had no intentions of ever getting married anyway...

"I need to show you this," he told Shelby, cutting off his thoughts. He ushered her toward the TV in the adjoining sitting area.

She sank onto the only furniture in the room, a two-seater couch a buddy had donated to the cause. "Nice house." Her voice held a question about his sparse decorating style.

"I haven't had time to do much furnishing," he told her.

Her glance at the curtainless windows said she'd noticed. "I'd offer you my card, but I've already given you one." The twinkle in her eye hinted that decorating his house was one "everything" job she'd

44

do gladly. "I'm a nester by instinct," she added as a sales pitch.

Forewarned is forearmed, Nick thought and reminded himself he was offering her a job, not a lifetime commitment. "I'm not sure how long I'll be here." He inserted the tape in the VCR. "I received this last night," he told her, "shortly after I learned of my grandfather's death."

She assumed a studious frown as he punched the Play button.

"I think this is a copy of the old man's last will and testament," he said.

She reacted with a startled "Oh" as the first of the still photos was displayed.

"These are of me and my mother."

"Ah. You wanted to show me your baby pictures? I'm touched."

She obviously resorted to wisecracks when she wasn't sure what else to do. They made him smile. She might even make this whole ordeal bearable.

He started to hit the Fast Forward but she stopped him with a hand over his on the remote control. "It'll probably make more sense if I see all of it, don't you think?"

"Maybe."

"Besides," she teased as he turned into a chubby, curly-haired three-year-old on screen. "You were adorable."

"Thanks," he said dryly, then sobered, "I think all this is just to let us know my grandfather kept up with what was going on in our lives."

"You didn't know these were being taken?" Her gaze flashed to his.

He shook his head and she looked back at the screen where a seven- or eight-year-old version of him was building a snowman. "I think my mother knew," he told her. It was one of the pieces that had fallen in place during the long restless night.

"Why do you think that?"

"This park, for one thing." He indicated the screen as the image changed. "That winter, for several weeks, Mom took me there in the snow almost every day."

Shelby frowned, not comprehending.

"She'd never taken me there before—it wasn't much of a park if I remember—just a few trees and a couple of swings and since we had a better swing set in our backyard, there wasn't much point. I remember thinking it strange that she would take me there in freezing weather when we had to bundle up to our eyeballs but she didn't when it was nice out."

"So she must have suspected someone was following you?"

It was his turn to nod.

"He kept tabs on you a couple of times each year," she said a few pictures later. She didn't take her eyes off the screen. "The pictures all seem to be in chronological order. Spring or summer, then fall or winter."

He was impressed with how observant she was. First the keyless entry to the garage, now this. The thought of having her on his side eased a heavy weight from his shoulders.

"My father isn't in any of them," he said pointedly, trying to keep the bitter taste in his mouth out of the words.

"I thought... Your parents are still married?"

"Were. He died a few years ago."

Her sympathy was cut short as the pictures changed to videos. Nick let her watch the rest of the personal glimpses without commentary.

"Oh." She sat up straighter when they got to the most recent one of him in jeans and an unbuttoned shirt, getting out of his pickup at a building site. "This totally ruins my image of you." She feigned disappointment. "I thought you were a rich playboy."

That one made him laugh aloud. "Where'd you get that idea?"

"You said the trip wasn't business." She regretfully tapped at the tear in his knee. "This suit isn't cheap."

"I only have one suit," he admitted. "I figured it should be a good one."

She nodded her agreement with his philosophy. "By the time you said you were going to a funeral, I guess the playboy image had stuck." She was obviously half-serious. "Even playboys go to funerals," she said pointedly.

"I build houses," he informed her.

"So I see. I suppose that explains the tan." She touched the tiny lines at the corner of one of his eyes. "And these. I figured you got them running around the Caribbean or some other exotic spot all winter."

"I earned every one of these." He scrubbed the

pleasant sensation of her touch from his crow's-feet with his little finger.

"This, too?" She nudged a knuckle into his muscled upper arm. "I thought you looked pretty healthy for a playboy. I blamed it on a gym."

Her casual nudges and touches and tracings brought all his senses to full alert. He drew a steadying breath.

His grandfather's voice brought their attention back to the TV. "This is the important part." He turned up the sound.

She looked from him to the tape, then back to him again, noting the resemblance between him and his grandfather.

Then she leaned closer and closer toward the TV, absorbed in what the old man was saying. Her mouth fell open at the point when the old man said he'd have to marry Christine. She didn't look at him again until it was finished. When she did, she was wide-eyed. "Your grandfather was nuts."

"That's why I need to get married."

She blinked twice. "So you're going to marry her?"

He realized he hadn't said a thing about his purpose in bringing her here. "I need to get married so I won't *have* to marry her." He rewound to the spot where his grandfather said, "Unless you're already married, of course" and played it twice. "On paper. Nice and legal. I need it signed, sealed and delivered. Today."

Her smile evaporated completely. At least she didn't look horrified by the idea. Just stunned. He found that reassuring. It said she was at least open to considering it. "You see why it's imperative? I hope maybe you—"

"You want me to find you a wife?" Her voice rose with each word.

Even with all she'd said about her business, it hadn't occurred to him that she'd suggest finding someone else. The idea of marrying anyone else was as intolerable as the thought of marrying Christine. "I want *you* to marry me." He corrected her. It would have to be to her.

She shook her head in disbelief. "Oh, Nick, you must be kidding."

"I'm as serious as a heart attack. Until this morning—when I ran into you," he offered by way of explanation, "I thought my only choice was marrying Christine if I didn't want Mom to miss out on her inheritance." The idea gave him tremors.

"Maybe your grandfather—"

"Is playing with my mother from the grave." He interrupted. "I plan to beat him at his own game."

"By getting married to someone else?"

He nodded. "Exactly."

Shelby kept her head down as she carved designs in the carpet with the toe of her shoe.

"What kind of person would let some old man pick a husband for her? If I wanted to get married, is that the kind of person I would choose? Why would she let herself be manipulated into marrying someone she hasn't even met?" he asked.

"For money," Shelby said almost to herself.

"Maybe she hopes I'll refuse. She has more to gain

if I *don't* marry her. She gets everything. Unless—"
He frowned.

Shelby waited for him to continue.

"I hadn't thought of it," he said, "but maybe
Christine sent the tape. She may have other plans for
her life, too. Maybe she's depending on me to get us
both out of a tough situation."

Shelby nodded in understanding. "So you think
you're doing her a favor, too? By marrying someone
else," she added as if he needed clarification.

"I *know* I'm doing her a favor. I'm giving her back
her life." Shelby had already proven her tendency to
worry about everyone else. It wasn't a bad attribute
to play to. "If I show up at the funeral married, my
mother and Christine inherit what should be theirs to
begin with—without any further effort on their part.
If I don't, no matter what happens with Christine,
Chester Celinski has driven a wedge between my
mother and me."

"But surely your mother wouldn't expect you to
go along with this."

"I'm nominated to be my grandfather's sacrificial
lamb." His fingers went to her face to smooth away
the wrinkle she seemed determined to permanently
engrave between her brows. "It's human nature to
resent someone who stops you from having the things
you want, especially if it should have been yours by
right. How can she not resent me if I have it in my
power to give her her inheritance and refuse? And I'll
come to resent Mom if I marry Christine."

"So you need a wife," she said.

That word had him dropping his arm back to his

side. "I *need* to be married. I don't need a wife. There's a difference." He grinned. "You won't even have any wifely duties. Just your name on a piece of paper and some time—which I'll pay you for, of course."

"There has to be a way around this," she said, reaching for the remote to replay the tape.

"I did that a hundred times last night," he told her. "And there is a way around it," he said softly. "You're it."

"Surely there's a friend or something…"

He was shaking his head. "You think I could ask someone to do this as a favor? Think about it. Until you gave me the idea of hiring you, I was resigned to believing my only option was marrying Christine."

"Why?"

"As a friend, someone would be doing me a favor. A *big* favor. One that would have all sorts of emotional and legal strings attached. It'll only work if I can hire someone." She squirmed as he pinpointed in his gaze the exact "someone" he wanted to hire. "Do you know anyone else in the 'anything' business?"

She grinned, shaking her head, knowing she'd walked into this.

"So will you do it, Shelby? Will you marry me? As a job, of course," he added. "I want to hire you. I need H.E.L.P. Name your fee."

"Oh, Nick. I…I…" She eyed him speculatively. "So what do you get out of this?"

Of course. She'd expect some kind of settlement. Her share of the loot. And she'd deserve it. Money, either having it or not having it, had never been a guiding force in his life. He didn't think in terms of legal agreements and nonsensical clauses but he'd better now, he realized.

"How much is at stake here?" she asked when he didn't answer the first question right away.

In a million years, he never would have suspected the smell of money would be the thing that convinced her. He felt as if someone had gut-punched him. For some reason, the real financial implications had never struck him. Which was silly, he chided himself. What kind of business deal wasn't based on money? He'd planned to use H.E.L.P. services. For some fee.

"I really don't know," he admitted. "It's a lot— my dad used to say my grandfather was 'filthy rich,' but further than that, I don't know. And I can't commit what isn't mine," he added a not-so-subtle warning. "Mom is the one who'll inherit it, not me. So..." He shrugged. It hadn't occurred to him that he maybe couldn't afford her.

"What will you do after?" she asked, changing the subject. "Will you change your life?"

He frowned. "Probably in small ways and maybe in larger ways eventually, but..." He shrugged.

"You're going to keep on building houses?"

For a woman who could make him laugh so easily, it was the funniest thing she'd said all day. "I have no intention of changing anything I'm doing now," he told her. She seemed content with his answer. He put the knowledge away to think about later and looked at his watch.

"So name your price," he said. "What's your fee? I'll try to come up with it."

"You don't know how it's going to benefit you? That's not why you're doing it?" Her melodic voice broke into his thoughts.

"No," he replied.

Her smile returned. Her relieved sigh was as sincere as anything she'd done so far. "Good. That makes it easier."

He didn't understand.

"You want me to have an instant dollar figure answer when you can't answer the question yourself."

He shrugged. "The satisfaction I'll have has nothing to do with money," he assured her. "I refuse to be manipulated from the grave by a spiteful, vicious old man. And I like my mother," he added. "I want her to have what she should have—the kingdom my father used to joke about her giving up for him. He'd like it that I can do this for her."

Shelby used her lush mouth as if it were a dimmer switch, turning up the warmth in her green eyes as the corners of her lips curved up. "I want to help..."

"But..." He was suddenly exhausted with talking about this mess. Or maybe it was the tension. He wanted to talk and think about other things.

"How could we pull it off?"

"Then you're agreeing?"

"Give an inch, you'll take a mile," she asked with a wry smile, then sobered. "I'm asking for details. The specifics. To tell you the truth, even if I agree, it sounds impossible logistically. There are blood tests and waiting periods and we don't have time to go to Vegas or Reno, do we?"

"The bad news?"

She encouraged him to go on with raised eyebrows.

"I haven't worked out all the details. I need to make some phone calls. But there isn't much point if..." He put the question back on her.

"...if I don't agree," she finished for him.

He nodded. "I know you used to be able to get married in Miami, Oklahoma, in a day. No waiting period. I need to see if that's still legal. Miami's three or four hours one way if we drive, an hour or so if I can charter a plane. There may be limited business hours we have to work around. We just have to get it done in their required time frame and try to make it to the funeral."

"You promised your mother."

"So I need to get this process started."

She groaned and lowered her head in her hands. "How can I think when I'm so tired I can't see?" She leaned back into the small couch, closing her eyes tightly.

"I'll let you sleep on the way to Oklahoma," he promised softly. "If it makes you feel any better, I didn't get much sleep, either."

"Thinking about all this?"

He grinned ruefully. "I didn't come up with a single solution to my problems. I should have slept."

"You should have made a list of friends. Surely you know someone..."

"No one I'd trust," he said quietly.

"How do you know you can trust me?" Her wide-eyed gaze held his.

"We're talking business. It isn't personal. There's a difference."

"Your girlfriend would take you getting married personally," she said with a dash of humor he found disarming.

"If you're asking if I'm involved with someone, the answer is no. Nothing steady. And you?" He tossed back the question. Come to think of it, he didn't want some big brute running around, intent on killing him for marrying his girlfriend.

"Nobody I would consider good husband material," she said regretfully.

"Except me," he countered, then realized she hadn't really answered the question.

Her sidelong look at him said his attempt at humor was weak. She sighed and stared back at the ceiling. Nick didn't think she was seeing it. "Look. Do you have any other ideas? You said you hadn't turned down a job yet. How 'bout I just hire you to solve my problem? Tell me another option. I'll go along with whatever solution you come up with."

She turned her most frank gaze on him. "You think you have me pegged, don't you?"

"I hope I do."

She groaned.

"And I hope you're still feeling indebted to me for risking my neck for you this morning."

"That's blackmail," she accused lightly.

"Is it working?"

"I don't know. But if you use it," she warned with a grin, "you put this squarely in the favor column— not business. And that comes with all sorts of emotional strings attached," she reminded him.

"You're the one who said you owe me. I just believe people should pay their debts."

She winced and looked at him helplessly. "My big mouth gets me into so much trouble."

He could see why. It was wide and full, a very intriguing, inviting mouth if he'd ever seen one, and he'd seen a few in his time. In fact, he realized, he'd rather be doing lots of things with her besides worrying about getting married. Tasting and exploring those lips was only the beginning.

"I do feel obligated. I do know I owe you a *big* favor. But you'd best decide whether you're asking for a favor or want to keep this strictly business."

"I guess I was thinking of it as both," he admitted. He stood suddenly, as impatient with his thoughts as he was becoming with her. The minute hand on his watch seemed to speed up every time he looked at it. "Look," he paused, waiting for her to look at him, "you said you didn't have anything to do today. Go along with me for the ride. Pretend it's a lark, another adventure. Let me start the process and we'll iron out the finer details and anything else you want on the way. If you decide, even up to the last minute, that you don't want to go through with marrying me, I'll understand."

She pressed a hand dramatically to her breasts, as if he was leaving her breathless. He didn't need Shelby to bring attention to one of her most noticeable assets. "I have to go home. Change."

She grabbed her purse—the purse he'd recovered for her—and jumped up. "I have to—"

He caught her hand. "Is that a yes?" he asked

softly. Her worry about tiny little molehills—like the way she looked, which was perfect—while disregarding the mountains—like whether she should marry him at all—amused and beguiled him.

She opened her mouth but no sound came.

He taunted the silence with a finger to her lips. "Don't tell me you're speechless?"

She nodded as if she couldn't believe it herself.

"Surely you keep clothes for every occasion in your office." He saw nothing wrong with the jeans she had on but figured she would grant him one of her extravagant smiles. He could become addicted to them.

"Actually I *do* have something in my car," she told him arrogantly and laughed at his surprise. "The dress I wore to the anniversary party last night. I changed into this when I started the clean up. Are you afraid if you let me out of your sight that I'll leave and won't come back?"

"It didn't occur to me." He realized with a bit of amazement that he did trust her. "Should I worry?"

"No," she said and looked down at her hands.

"Does this mean you've decided you're going to marry me?"

"It means," she said hurriedly, as if she had to get the words out fast or she was afraid she'd change her mind, "I'm going to go with you." She took a breath that further inflated and drew attention again to her lush breasts. He forced his gaze not to linger.

"Then go home, take care of anything you need to. I need about an hour to make some phone calls, work out those details you're so worried about. And then I'll be ready. Can you be?''

She nodded silently, grimaced and muttered something about dog food. She started to turn and go. She stopped midstep.

''You sound like you expect me to go with you to the funeral. Does that mean you don't want people to know it's fake? Does it make any difference?''

Legally Nick didn't *think* it made a difference. But uncertainty made him frown. And there was the added mystery of the tape. Who *had* sent it? Would someone—maybe Christine—be in trouble for the advance warning? The more he thought about it, the more convinced he became that Christine had to be the one who sent the tape. Who else would have anything to gain or lose if he arrived for the reading of his grandfather's Will with or without a wife?

''We might have to answer fewer questions if we let it look real.'' He thought of his mother's reaction and amended the statement. ''At least fewer questions from my grandfather's lawyers.''

''And we could be vague about when we actually 'eloped,''' Shelby suggested.

''Can you go with me to St. Louis?''

She lifted a shoulder. ''If I'm going to do it, I want to do it well. I like to do *any* job I take well.'' Her grin tilted to a captivating angle. ''So I guess I also need to pack a bag.''

He could almost see her mind clicking through some sort of mental list.

She held up one cautionary finger. ''I'll hold you

to the promise of an escape clause if I decide I can't
go through with any of it."

"Deal," he accepted, holding out his hand.

"Deal," she agreed.

The hand she put in his felt like a lifeline. He didn't
release it. He felt like kissing it. Or her upturned lips.
Instead he tapped one of the cute little freckles on her
cute little nose. "See you in an hour. Okay?"

"Okay," she whispered.

CHAPTER FOUR

FORTY-FIVE minutes later, Nick knew a lot more about what they had to do and how much time they had to do it in. He changed out of his ruined suit, finger-brushed his teeth—his toothbrush was still in his car. After finding his spare keys so they could stop by the grocery store and get his bag, he settled on the porch step to wait for Shelby's return. When a half hour had gone by and she hadn't returned, he started to worry whether she'd chickened out.

With a little more time, he worried that she hadn't.

Damn! What in the hell was he doing? What did he really know about Shelby Wright? What he did know—for the most part—made him smile. What he didn't terrified him. He'd seen her self-sufficient and arrogant; quaking like a leaf and yelling at him to cover her fright; observant and problem-solving; caring and compassionate. In a few short hours, he felt like he knew her well. But was that possible?

A honking horn disrupted his thoughts and he turned, expecting to see Shelby's little white car. Seeing his own stopped him in his tracks. Sleek and low to the ground, the sporty two-seater glittered wickedly in the bright sun.

Shelby got out of the driver's seat and dangled his keys in his direction. She proudly dropped them into his outstretched hand as he met her in front of the hood. "Nice car," she said, patting the polished black exterior. "Lots of muscle."

He inwardly cringed and resisted the urge to use the tail of his shirt to wipe away her fingerprints. At least she appreciated it. He'd actually dated one or two women who'd had the temerity to hint that if things got a little bit serious, it would have to go.

He was never sure if they didn't like it because it didn't look remotely like a family car—and that's what they had in mind—or if they were afraid he'd attract too much attention from other women. Things had gotten *un*serious quickly.

With Shelby, he was torn between terror that she'd been driving his baby and pleasure that somehow she'd managed to solve one more problem. "How…"

"I had to go right past the store on my way home," she explained. "I saw your car, thought it might be worth stopping to look for your keys." She looked smug. "I walked down the side of the store where you'd chased that guy and there they were, right in broad daylight."

He added resourceful to his growing list of her assets. He couldn't keep the relief from his voice, "I haven't let myself think about my car and the keys just lying there on the ground. I kept reminding myself that's why I pay those high insurance premiums."

"Well, now you don't have to worry."

"Thanks."

Shelby had changed to some longish, whitish, gauzy kind of dress that gave shadowy glimpses of her perfect form beneath when she moved. The neck dipped into a V, leaving hints of exquisite treasure

without really showing him a thing. It taunted and
intrigued him and fired his imagination. He shook his
head to rid himself of erotic images taking shape there
and forced his thoughts back to priorities.

"What'd you do with your car?" he asked.

"Left it at home. It's only a block and a half to the
store so I walked back and got your car."

"You carried your bag—"

"I dropped back by my duplex and picked up my
suitcase after I got your car." She swung a thumb
toward the trunk. "It's in there. With yours," she
added with satisfaction.

"Good." Another glimpse of Shelby. Efficient.
Attentive to details. He cleared his throat. "Shall we
go?"

Shelby settled in the passenger seat as he readjusted
his seat far enough away from the steering wheel to
drive. Those long, elegant legs weren't quite as long
as he'd imagined. And staring at them wasn't getting
them where they needed to go.

"Would it be too much to ask where we're going?"
she asked—much too cheerfully.

He tromped on the nervous thought. There was no
reason to be suspicious because she was being pleasant about this whole thing. Would he prefer that she
was grumpy and grudging?

"The downtown airport," he answered her question. "I managed to charter a plane."

She grimaced. "Ouch. Isn't that terribly expen-
sive?"

"That's why I have credit cards," he said. "If
nothing else, I can get a loan from my rich mother

once she's firmly reestablished as the heiress princess.''

Shelby laughed as he hoped she would. And he felt pleased with himself for sneaking in a reminder that he wouldn't have direct access to whatever inheritance was at stake.

"We're going to Miami, Oklahoma. I called. Nothing's changed. We can still get married there without a waiting period and get back here in time to catch an early flight for St. Louis in the morning. I made those arrangements, too.''

"We should be fine then, shouldn't we?" She looked to him for confirmation.

"The pilot I hired said he'd have everything ready to go by the time we get to the airport. I told him we would be there around eleven." He checked the clock on the dashboard. "We're half an hour behind, but we should still be in Miami by two or so. We can get there as late as four-thirty to do the deed.''

"You think of it that way? As 'doing the deed'?" He took his eyes off the road to question her. "Somehow, you make getting married sound positively horrid.''

He bit his tongue and reminded himself she could still back out at any time. "You aren't exactly jumping up and down at the opportunity. I haven't heard a definite yes yet.''

"It's not the most romantic marriage proposal I've ever had,'' she admitted with a grin, then eyed him speculatively. "And it sure isn't what I envisioned.''

He had a feeling the dreamy look on her face indicated she was having a fantasy now.

"So you're one of those confirmed bachelors?" It was half question, half statement.

"Hey. I proposed, didn't I?"

She laughed. "You weren't exactly jumping up and down with joy," she modified his phrase. "Don't you eventually want a home? Family?"

"I have both," he said pointedly.

"Family?"

"My mom, a few aunts, uncles and cousins on my father's side. You only have to sit down around a holiday table once with all of them to know I have enough family for anybody," he said dryly.

She wrinkled her nose at his idea of home and family. It definitely didn't coincide with hers. "Is that what you want?" he asked.

"Yes." Her green eyes shone. Her mouth tilted at the one corner. "I want the traditional kind of thing," she admitted. "A husband. Kids. The same thing I saw in those pictures of you growing up."

"You? Traditional?"

"In my own kind of way," she defended.

"Without a father in the picture." He pointed out what had been missing from those glimpses of his life.

"Even though your grandfather didn't include him in the pictures, you could tell he was there," she said. "Your mother's eyes glowed with contentment. You looked happy. Someone was very obviously in the background, lovingly supporting that take-life-as-it-comes life-style your mother and you seemed to have," she added.

"That family could have been independently

wealthy," he suggested. "If I hadn't already told you—"

"It wasn't *that* lush a life-style," she said dryly.

"And that's what you want?"

She nodded. "I just haven't found the right man. Yet," she added.

"You're working to build a business just to let it go bust the minute you find some man to support you?"

"No," she said indignantly. "Why do you think I want to establish my business? Most women have to work these days and it's exactly the kind of thing that will fit in and around my family. Perfectly."

That gave him food for thought. She talked about her dream family as if it was reality. It made him see her in a whole new—scary—light.

She chewed at the corner of her lip. "Frankly that's one thing that worries me." He didn't think she even noticed his frown. "I don't want to ruin my future on a whim."

"What do you mean?"

She flushed slightly and looked down at the hands she'd folded in her lap. "This will change things. I have to consider any long-term consequences."

"Such as..."

"I'll be a divorcée. Some men wouldn't want another man's discard," she said. "I need to think about stuff like that."

He managed to laugh. "I'll let you do the discarding. How's that?"

"Thanks," she said. "But that's not the point."

"I'll sign a written statement, explaining everything. We can have it notar—"

"Stop." Her voice interrupted with a sudden urgency.

Nick's heart came to his throat. He thought he'd flunked some kind of shall-I-go-through-with-this test. But when he looked at Shelby, she was waving toward the towering concrete walls of the area's largest mall. The exit was coming up. "We have to stop and buy you a suit," she explained more calmly. "We may not get another chance. It won't take long," she assured him.

He'd changed into jeans and a knit polo shirt.

She obviously had no intention of marrying him dressed as he was. But then he hadn't expected her to turn up dressed as a garden party bride. The only thing missing was flowers in her hair. He frowned. What? Did women who were hooked on some marriage fantasy keep a perfect dress hanging in their closets at all times? Just in case?

"We may not get another chance," she repeated.

He turned on his blinker. He wasn't ready to risk her backing out because he wasn't appropriately attired. "You're right," he said. "Miami's not a very big town. We're more likely to find something suitable—" he liked his unconscious pun and checked to see if she caught it as he swung into the exit lane "—here."

She rolled her eyes, but smiled. "We may not have time later today," she said. "Do you know what time the funeral is tomorrow?"

"I only know it's tomorrow," he admitted, feeling

like a fool. She wasn't worried about the wedding. She was concerned about his wardrobe for the funeral. She thought of everything. She boggled his mind.

"Thanks for thinking for me," he muttered. "I'm obviously not."

She pointed him to the right entrance to the mall, promising him that the best store to find exactly what he needed was just inside.

He parked in the still almost empty lot. There weren't many people shopping this early on a Friday morning.

And he'd better start considering future consequences himself, he thought as she ushered him toward the huge building. He'd better be thinking about an escape hatch out of this mess. So far he'd been so concerned about getting into it that he hadn't considered getting out.

How in the hell did she know what men's store was the best? Shelby Wright was much too good at wifely things to make him comfortable. It was starting to give him the heebie-jeebies.

Shelby talked under her breath a lot, Nick discovered. It would have been amusing if he couldn't hear what she was saying. She mumbled about his too broad chest and too slim waist and suggested he was a mismatched size as she pushed hangers around on the rack. Just when he was beginning to feel deformed, she pulled out a black suit with a tiny, almost unnoticeable white pinstripe and deemed the cut perfect for his "perfect" physique. She flushed and wouldn't meet his eyes when he grinned.

She berated herself for not thinking ahead when the

clerk offered their free tailoring service for the pants hem. "I knew I should have brought my car," she grumbled quietly as she made him stop at the discount store to buy tape so she could "hem" them for him some vague "sometime."

She called herself all kinds of a fool as they climbed into the plane at the airport, then cursed her stupidity as she fastened herself into the seat.

"This is the silliest thing I've ever done," she finally said directly to him when she had to shout to be heard over the engine.

"It's a business decision," he called back, glad to have the chance to point out once again that this was business. "A good business decision," he added.

"It'll be easier to talk once we're in the air," Don, the pilot, assured them over his shoulder. "The noise will be a little less."

Shelby looked meaningfully from Nick to the back of Don's head. Don obviously had practice at hearing over the roar. Nick, who'd crawled into the back seat with her, claimed her hand between both of his and assured her he'd explained everything to Don. He was glad she didn't try to withdraw her hand. "Do you like flying?"

"I've never flown in anything but a commercial jet." She lifted one shoulder. "I guess I'll find out."

"It was a hobby of my dad's," Nick told her. "He loved anything that would fly."

After the early-morning chill, the day had settled into one of those brilliant spring days. Nick's mood suddenly matched it. He was going to win! Beat his grandfather at his own game.

The takeoff was smooth, almost exhilarating. As Don had promised, the noise settled from a small roar to a loud hum.

As soon as they were on a steady course, Shelby blinked sleepily and pulled her hand from his to cover a yawn.

"You ready to talk details, Shelby," he started. "I'll certainly feel better when we get a few more things nailed down."

"You promised me a nap," she said.

"Soon," he promised, but noticed the shadows under her eyes were growing deeper. "We also need to discuss how long."

"What?"

"Six months ought to be long enough, I'm guessing. Maybe less. Six months will give us time to cover any legal bases that need covering. And if anyone is going to contest the Will, they will surely make a move in that length of time. Will that be all right? You can dump me in six months?"

Her eyelids drooped lazily. "What if I don't want to?" she said. "I'm kidding." She held up both hands in protest then reiterated it as she smothered another yawn.

And what he'd taken as a flirtatious batting of eyelashes a minute ago was her way of fighting off sleep.

"I thought it was funny," she said when he still didn't say anything and shrugged as if his sense of humor might be severely lacking. "We can probably get it annulled," she offered. Her body drooped against him and began to match her heavy eyelids. "We shouldn't have to get a divorce," she added when he frowned, "since we won't even be living together...let alone having sex."

Don's head straightened and he leaned further back in his seat. Nick hoped he wasn't hard of hearing. It would be a shame if he missed this part of the conversation.

"I think whether or not a marriage is consummated is part of the criteria for an annulment."

"Whatever." Her body felt warm and comfortably stable against his. "But you know it will be difficult to get a divorce settlement if you don't get a divorce?"

She laughed that husky laugh and let her head fall slightly back. "I get the house," she mumbled.

He got a wonderful view of the long, flawless line of her throat. The tender spot beneath her ear beckoned him. It drove most women crazy if you kissed them there.

It drove him crazy thinking about driving her crazy. She fascinated him. She tantalized him. He hoped she didn't notice what she was doing to him. He intently tried to think of what other bases they needed to cover so they wouldn't have a mismanaged mess on their hands when it was time to end their "silly" marriage. She wanted the house? It might be worth it if he needed to go that route.

He wished they had time to see a lawyer, get some sort of written agreement between them. But since it was a choice between trusting her and beating his grandfather at his own game, he'd choose trusting her anytime. "Seriously, we need to talk about money. What do you want out of this?"

She made a face. "I haven't exactly priced this kind of service before." Her grin disappeared as she explained as if by rote, "I charge differently for a job I can do from home than what I charge for other things."

"What do you mean?"

"Like finding a busy couple a plumber they can trust. Someone who can do the job when they need it done." The last words were drawn out in the midst of another gaping yawn. "I charge a small hourly fee for that with a minimum of one hour. If I have to leave my house—go to their house and *wait* to let the plumber in, for example—" she drew her feet up onto the narrow seat and rearranged her flowing skirt around her "—I charge a higher rate and bill them a minimum of three hours." She settled her bent knees across his legs.

"I finally understand," he said.

Her brows rose.

"What you actually do," he answered the semi-interested query in her eyes, "You do the types of things people don't have time to do themselves."

"Or the things they wouldn't or couldn't," she added.

"Or things no one else would…like marry a total stranger."

"Like marry a total stranger," she repeated so quietly he had to lip-read over the noise of the plane. She was suddenly somber. And then she yawned, noisily this time. "I'm so tired, I can't think. Please. Would you mind if I took a little nap?"

"We have to settle this," he said in a practical tone

but turned in the seat accommodatingly and put his
arm around her and patted his shoulder. She thumped
it twice, like a pillow, then leaned into it.

"Later," she sighed. She yawned again and closed
her eyes. "I can't keep my eyes open any longer and
I assume you want me standing on my own two feet
when we get married..." her voice trailed off.

He smiled. "We wouldn't want people thinking I
drugged and dragged you, kicking and screaming into
this." He didn't think she heard that or his "Go to
sleep, Shelby."

He wondered if she knew she'd said "when" not
"if." He looked down at her peaceful face, pulled her
closer and smiled again.

The little plane landed with a jolt at the small airport
on the edge of Miami an hour later. Shelby was snoring softly and he looked down, expecting the thud to
wake her. Her hand just slid further down his chest,
making him tingle in anticipation of where it would
be next if the plane jolted again.

He scowled at his sudden impulse to kiss her awake
and shook her gently instead. "Wake up, Shelby."

Her green eyes opened and stared blankly into his
as Don brought the small four-passenger plane to a
complete stop. He gave her the minute she needed to
get her bearings. He knew she'd found them when a
startled awareness widened her eyes. With a smile of
appreciation mixed with chagrin, she reached up to
cup his face in her palm. "You make a good pillow,"
she said quietly.

And she made an appealing package. He cleared his throat. "Ready?"

She nodded and started worrying about repairing her makeup. With Don's assurance that he'd be waiting when they returned and his skeptical "Good luck" ringing in their ears, they made their way into the tiny airfield terminal.

"I should have worn my new suit," Nick apologized when she came out of the bathroom all primped and glossed.

"Your pants weren't hemmed," she reminded him amiably. "I just did what I felt comfortable with," she added. "You did the same. Don't you think that's how it's supposed to work?"

"You're going to make someone a lovely bride," he complimented, tongue-in-cheek.

She chuckled at his obvious attempt to reassure them both that this wasn't real and dropped him an old-fashioned curtsy. "Thank you, kind sir."

"You've done me proud," he added sincerely.

"I take every bit of H.E.L.P. seriously," she said as he offered her his arm. "Now. How are we going to get to town?"

He led her out the front of the building, opposite where they'd come in. "I made arrangements to rent a car," Nick told her and held up the keys he'd picked up at the desk inside while she was doing whatever she did to put that provocative gleam back into her eyes. "Shall we see if we can find it?"

The car was there and because the town was small and the airport manager had been more than detailed with his directions, within ten minutes, they were parking in front of an imposing, official-looking courthouse.

Nick felt weary as he turned off the engine. Butterflies took flight in his stomach. Technically, all they had to do was say a few words and sign their names to a small piece of paper. But legally, they'd be married.

He'd be tied to her. And she to him...for better or for worse, the words popped into his head.

He took a deep breath and held out a hand to her as soon as they both reached the sidewalk in front of the car. He pointed toward the park bench beneath a big tree halfway up the wide sidewalk leading to the large native stone building. "You want to stop and catch our breath?"

She compressed her lips and shook her head. "Don't give me a chance to think about this," she warned lightly.

"That's my problem," he admitted. "I've had too much time to think."

The sun slid behind a cloud and she shivered. "We've come this far. What's one step further?" She glanced at the sky, which had become a rolling, moving mass of gray. "I just hope that's not an omen," she remarked, half under her breath.

"A good omen," he assured her.

"The sun is supposed to shine on your wedding day," she said dryly, "not run behind a cloud the minute you get ready to go through with it." Her stomach growled as if adding its own dire warning.

"Your stomach's doing flip-flops, too?" Nick asked sympathetically.

"What my stomach's doing has nothing to do with nerves," Shelby told him. "I'm starving. Do you realize we've had nothing to eat today? At least I haven't, and I don't know when you could have."

The hollow feeling in his gut probably had as much to do with hunger as nerves, Nick realized. "Tell you what," he promised, lifting her chin with one finger because he suddenly had to touch her, "after we get the license and blood tests, we'll have a half hour's wait for the results. We'll find something to eat then. Okay?"

"Great. There should be some rule about getting married on an empty stomach. It sounds to me like it would be really bad luck."

He cast a look at the sky. "And if the sun refuses to come back out of hiding, we'll just wait for it."

Her melodious laughter washed over him. "I've always dreamed of some man promising me the moon." She rolled her eyes. "So what do I get? One who offers me the sun. Somehow, it just isn't quite the same." She wrinkled her nose. "Is there no justice?"

"You won't be sorry," he promised as they started up the walk toward the courthouse and hoped she didn't notice that he said it as much for him as her.

"They must do quite a marriage business here," Nick commented as they returned outdoors ten minutes later with the required paperwork in his hands. He hoped she wouldn't notice the sun still hadn't come back out from behind the clouds. If anything, everything had grown darker and clouds were scuttling ominously across the sky.

"She sure had it all down pat, didn't she?" Shelby referred to the woman who had helped them.

He pointed across the street. A sign in front of an older two-story frame house announced the wedding chapel. It was only a few yards from Oklahoma Serology where they had to get their blood tests. "You can walk from the courthouse to the blood tests to the Chapel without ever leaving sight of your car."

Everyone was as efficient as the physical arrangement was. Within minutes, the phlebotomist was done taking their blood.

Nick escorted Shelby back outside. "Now lunch?" And they'd use the time to dot the *i*'s and cross the *t*'s. He definitely wanted in, but he also wanted to know how they were going to get out and what it would cost him.

Shelby's smile looked much too content. "Now lunch."

CHAPTER FIVE

SHELBY vetoed several fast-food places and a couple of specialty restaurants with a variety of grimaces. Nick decided she was one of those delicate, picky eaters. He pulled into the parking lot of a twenty-four-hour coffee shop type restaurant attached to a motel. "Take what you get or weep," his father used to say. If she turned up her nose at this one, Nick was prepared to borrow it.

"How's this?" he asked, turning off the car. "I'll bet they have a varied selection."

"Fine." She pushed a strand of the gold-brown hair back from her face. He watched one elegant finger hook it behind her delicate ear.

Then she amused and surprised him by ordering the biggest steak on the menu. "I thought you were a picky eater," he commented after he'd ordered the same thing.

"I'm hungry," she protested. "You kept choosing fast-food places and I was afraid you weren't really going to feed me." Then she laughed.

"What's so funny?"

Her brows furrowed in concern. "I was starting to feel indignant that I'd agreed to marry someone who didn't care a thing about what I wanted." She shook her head as if to clear it. "We sounded just like my parents when they're trying to come to an agreement on something. I feel so silly," she said softly. "I feel like a little kid, playing dress-up with my mom's clothes. Only it isn't her clothes I'm trying on this time." She leaned conspiratorially forward and whispered, "It's her...her...life," she found the word she wanted.

He grinned back and leaned forward, his hands slightly pitched between them. "I just had one of my father's thoughts. Scary, isn't it?"

She laughed. The waitress looked at them knowingly as she placed salads in front of them. "I'll bet Rita thinks we're here to get married," Shelby whispered as soon as the woman left.

"What makes you think her name's Rita?"

"You think she's wearing someone else's name tag?"

He suddenly felt as giddy as she was acting. Anyone listening or watching would suspect they'd had too much to drink. "Maybe. Maybe she wants to be someone different today, too."

"You wish you were someone different right now?" Shelby asked as Rita returned with their salads.

He didn't know how to answer. He took a bite of his salad and lifted his free hand helplessly. "You realize, for all intents and purposes, we don't know each other?"

She nodded and chewed. "It feels like I know you," she said at last.

"Maybe it's our shared experiences?"

She squinted contemplatively.

He found himself smiling again like a goofy kid.

"Buying panty hose? Intimate experience." He listed the items. "Recovering your purse? Intimate experience."

"Asking—or being asked—to marry someone," she offered. "Intimate experience."

"Fixing and buying clothes. Intimate experience." He glanced down at his clothes. "I should have left that suit on. Then Rita could suspect you've been trying to tear my clothes off."

Her laughter was throaty, relaxed, pleasant. He liked it and wished she *would* tear off his clothes. Intimate experience.

"You realize I know more about my "mother-in-law" and your grandfather than I know about know you," she said suddenly serious.

He pushed his salad to one side as the waitress brought their steaks. Conversation stopped while they told her what else they needed and dressed their baked potatoes.

His stomach growled loudly as he took his first bite and Shelby's smile grew. "No wonder you were getting impatient with me."

"You could tell?"

"I didn't have a clue until you snarled at me," she said facetiously. "That's when I started getting indignant."

"Okay, Ms. Indignant Shelby Wright, what else do you want to know before you marry me?" he asked before popping a bite of steak into his mouth.

"I think it might be handy to know where my soon-to-be husband grew up. Did he have a happy childhood...stuff like that."

"My dad was in the service—that's how Mom and Dad met—until I was almost eight, so we moved around a lot. Then we settled on his family farm halfway between Lawrence and Shawnee Mission, where he grew up. I spent the rest of my growing up years there and now I'm in Kansas City.''

"Brothers and sisters?''

"No.'' He shook his head.

"That's sad,'' she said.

"You have some?''

"I'll share,'' she said, pleased. "You'll have a brother-in-law in the Army, stationed in Germany; and a sister-in-law in the wilds of Nebraska. She's married to a farmer and has three kids of her own now.''

"And your parents?''

"Your future mother- and father-in-law?''

Put like that, he wasn't sure he wanted to know. She was beginning to make him nervous again.

"They recently retired.'' Her face lit as she thought of them. "They like to travel and are doing a lot of it.'' She sighed. "They're in Europe now, plan on being there another six weeks. They used my brother as an excuse to go.''

"You sound like you miss them.''

"A lot,'' she admitted.

"And how will they feel about your marriage?''

Her fork hovered in midair. "I hadn't thought about them.'' She frowned. "They're going to think I've gone off the deep end and done one more foolish, impulsive thing.'' She savored another piece of the steak thoughtfully.

"That's normal for you, I take it," he said.

"Far too normal. It got me in way too much trouble while I was growing up." She shook her head. "For the first time since they left," she said, referring to her parents again, "I think I'm glad they're gone." She brightened. "By the time they get back, it may be over. Right?"

He'd said six months. It irritated him that she seemed to be in a bigger hurry to get rid of him than he was of her. But sharing in-laws and out-laws would bring complications they didn't need. It would probably be better if it was over by the—

"Shoot, if it's over by then, I may not even tell them." She broke into his thoughts. She gnawed the corner of her lip. "I may not bother them with this bit of information if it's past history when they get back."

It rankled that she might be unwilling to tell them she was married to him. He could give her a long list of women who would consider him a good catch. And it irked him to feel that way. He couldn't have it both ways. "You talk to them regularly?"

"E-mail, when they can get connected. Dad took his little laptop computer."

"What about you?" he changed the subject. "You said why you chose the business you're in, but you didn't say how you came up with the idea."

"The company I worked for promoted me to an administrative assistant and I ended up doing a little bit of everything. Usually the stuff that no one else wanted to mess with."

"Like?"

"Planning company picnics. Dropping everything to take a rush order to the printers. You know. Everything. My full-time job ended up being 'Give it to Shelby. She'll do anything.' I found I really liked it."

"So you decided to go into business doing something similar for yourself."

"I wish I was that adventurous," she protested. "I'm not."

She was every bit that adventurous. Adventurous enough that she was here in Miami, Oklahoma, less than an hour away from marrying a man she'd known less than twelve hours. He thanked his lucky stars for their chance meeting at the grocery store.

Shelby explained her decision to go into business for herself when the company relocated to Indiana. She had a choice of going there or losing the job she liked.

"And you didn't want to leave your family?"

"My folks live in Emporia," she said. "About a hundred miles southwest?"

He nodded. "I've driven through it."

"I didn't necessarily want to move that far away, but my parents weren't the reason."

A man, Nick thought. She wanted to stay for some man.

She didn't mention any such thing. "I just realized I wanted to continue doing what I'd been doing, only for myself. I needed the nudge of my job disappearing to come up with the idea, let alone make the decision to do it. And starting a business where you already know people is twice as easy as starting somewhere where you don't.''

"Not to mention that there was no reason to move if you weren't going for the job," Nick said pointedly.

"Good point," she congratulated him as if the thought would have never occurred to her. "How'd you get started in the construction business? Did you work for someone else and then decide you wanted to go out on your own?"

"Not exactly." He pushed his plate aside and reached for the coffee cup Rita had just filled.

"I was a schoolteacher," he confided. The normal response was a stunned and doubting "You?" He'd admit he didn't look like a teacher and most people decided he was a football coach or PE teacher.

Shelby didn't react at all. "You didn't like that?" She took another bite of her baked potato.

He shrugged. "It was a combination of things. Mostly, it got too complicated."

"What'd you teach?"

"Fifth grade."

"Fifth grade?" A little of the surprise crept into her voice.

"And I coached the junior high football team," he admitted.

"What got complicated?"

"I probably should have been teaching third grade," he said. "I think the kids got too old for me. They outgrew me."

Her sweet smile drew his gaze. At least he thought those lips would be sweet. Dessert. The thought came from nowhere. Kissing her would be excellent dessert.

"So how did that lead you into building houses?"

He sucked in a deep breath and regrouped. "That's what I did in the summers." He lifted a shoulder and flexed his muscles. "It got me outside, kept me in shape."

She tilted her head back, appraising them. "You wear those sexy leather tool belts with hammers and stuff all over the place?" she asked, a mock huskiness in her voice.

"Sometimes," he drawled. She was playing. It was supposed to be fun. But the air between them sizzled with an almost palpable, physical energy. It felt heavy and made him lethargic. He couldn't keep his gaze from her mouth. And he wanted dessert more than ever.

"And those tight white T-shirts?"

"White gets too dirty."

"Darn." She snapped her fingers and sighed her disappointment. Her second sigh wasn't orchestrated. She looked away and concentrated on taking a huge gulp of water.

"I could get some white T-shirts," he volunteered.

"Let me know when you do?" She laughed and the tension between them eased. "So you built houses in the summer to keep in shape?"

"It started out as a summer job, three months of the year my junior and senior year of college. The man I worked for was my best friend's father." Now his mouth seemed to move woodenly. "I liked the job so kept on after I started teaching since I had most of the summer off every year." He shrugged again.

"When he died, his wife asked if I wanted to buy the business—"

"Why didn't he give it to his son?"

"His son's a doctor." Nick smiled. "He didn't want it. He did get half the money when I bought it. So...same difference?" he asked.

She nodded. "You don't miss teaching?"

"I miss some of the kids."

"Not the same thing?"

"Not at all."

"Maybe you should have some of your own."

"I don't think so. I don't picture myself as a father."

Shelby's small hand fisted under her chin as she propped her head on it. "Why?"

He wasn't sure why. He liked children, he just couldn't see himself having some of his own. "I don't know," he finally admitted. "I just don't see myself that way. Maybe I don't want the responsibility." The subject made him edgy.

He was relieved when Rita returned but her offer of dessert almost made him laugh out loud. As far as he was concerned, her selection of homemade pie just didn't compare. When they both declined, she left the check.

Shelby gathered her purse and looked at him expectantly.

"We still have to settle what you want out of this," he reminded her.

"We'd settled it."

"When?"

"On the plane. I thought you understood. I'll

charge my usual fee,'' she said blithely. "When you
need me, like today—I'm out of the house. The clocks
running. By the time we get home tonight, I'll have
in a good twelve, fourteen hours. It isn't going to be
a small bill,'' she cautioned him. "But I'll bill you
as I normally would.''

"That's hardly fair. If you're going to be more or
less—'' he searched for a word ''—on call,'' he finally found one.

"For what?''

He couldn't think of a thing. "I don't know,'' he
admitted. "Which is exactly my point. You should
get *something* out of this.''

"I am. My regular fee,'' she said in a matter-of-
fact voice.

He shook his head. "That's not enough.''

"I'm satisfied.''

"I'm asking you to make a legal commitment. To
put your life on hold.''

"Are you? I didn't hear *that* part of the bargain.''

"Not literally,'' he said irritably. "I just
mean…you know what I mean.''

"I don't, but I think I want to. If there's something
you expect that you haven't told me about, it would
probably be a good idea. Are you asking me not to
see anyone else?''

That question made him frown. He wasn't sure
what he wanted. "*That's* what I mean,'' he said and
suddenly knew the point he wanted to make. "I mean
if someone—someone you're seeing—asked you to
marry them, you couldn't exactly do it. Not right

away, anyway, could you? That puts your life on hold, so to speak.''

She waved his concern away with a sigh. ''That's not likely in the next six months. If I had someone I was even remotely considering in the picture right now, would I have made it *this* far?'' she asked.

''So you're not seeing anyone,'' he confirmed.

''I didn't say that.'' She corrected him with an impish grin. ''But believe me, I'm not seeing anyone I'd marry.''

''Oh. You're waiting for the classic white knight.''

''I'm picky,'' she contradicted almost apologetically, as if she couldn't help it.

He didn't know what to say to that so he reverted to the previous subject. ''Still, don't you think you ought to have a monthly allowance of some sort,'' he asked. ''For your trouble?''

''You mean like a separate maintenance allowance?''

''Yeah. No.'' He immediately changed his mind. Calling it something associated with marriage or divorce bothered him. He needed something…legal, businesslike. ''A retainer.''

She spread her hands again. ''Do you think?''

He nodded. ''A retainer.'' He was speaking legalese. He'd been thinking too many legal thoughts since last night. ''Then charge me your usual hourly fee for any actual time I require,'' he added, satisfied at last that they were both getting a fair shake. ''Like today, and over the weekend while we're in St. Louis. Deal?'' And she shouldn't have any reason to complain in the future.

This time, she was the first to stick out her hand. "Deal."

"Then let's go get this over with," he suggested.

"Thanks." She gingerly released his hand. "You make it sound like marrying me is worse than a prison sentence."

"If it's any comfort," he said, "I can think of worse things."

"Like?"

"Like?" He twisted his mouth as if it were impossible to think of anything worse. "Dental surgery, maybe?"

"Gee, thanks."

"Chasing down purse snatchers," he offered.

"Low blow," she said, holding up a warning finger. "I've already agreed to your little scheme. You don't need the blackmail."

"I guess you're right. And I can think of something much worse." It was all he could do not to shudder.

"Buying panty hose for your mother?"

He laughed. "Close."

She waited.

"Marrying Christine," he said, "would be much, much worse." He almost felt guilty for saying it. The woman couldn't be that bad considering she'd at least had the presence of mind to try to get them both out of this nightmare his grandfather had been determined to plunge them into—if she'd sent the tape, he reminded himself.

"Too bad I can't take that as a compliment," Shelby said ruefully.

"Would *you* willingly go along with marrying someone for no reason but financial gain?"

Shelby turned somber. "I think I'm doing exactly that."

He grabbed his heart dramatically. "I'm crushed. You've totally destroyed my self-esteem. Marrying me is such a hardship, it takes money *and* the repayment of a favor?"

Her reaction was just what he intended and her laughter lit her expressive eyes.

Who would have believed this getting married business could be fun? He stood and extended his hand. "Come on. I have a feeling we'd better get this over with before we both change our minds. Let's do it."

The ceremony was quick and nearly painless. In the minister's authoritative tone, the words sounded like they came from God himself. Shelby's eyes got bigger and bigger as she said her vows. Nick realized this wasn't easy for her.

He sighed with relief when the ceremony was over and regretted not getting her flowers.

"You may kiss the bride," the minister intoned, taking Nick by surprise. He hadn't thought far enough ahead to expect such a bonus.

Shelby was looking at him expectantly.

He could feel the other three people in the room, their witnesses, LaVerne and her husband, and the minister, waiting with quiet anticipation, too.

"Shelby," he said softly. "Shelby." Her lips tilted toward his. How his mouth could feel parched and thirsty, even though his mouth was watering like crazy, he didn't understand.

"Shelby," he whispered again and felt a dangerous walking-on-a-tightrope feeling creep up his spine.

Nick drew her close. She felt warm and solid. Holding her made the bizarre day seem suddenly grounded in reality while at the same time, unreal.

He savored the clean, pure scent of her. He enjoyed the subtle pressure of her breasts against his chest. Her hand fluttered against his heart and it sped up in response. His hands smoothed the soft fabric of her dress against her back, pulling her closer. The material imitated the whisper of sound taking the dress off her would. He banished the last thought from his mind and gave her the kiss the entire world seemed to be waiting for.

He didn't want to stop.

Her lips were warm and ripe. They froze momentarily then parted under his. Her soft intake of air robbed him of breath and he wasn't certain if he pulled her closer or if the increased sense of pressure against him came from her. Him, he decided, as her body seemed to change from something solid and real to something malleable and mystical in his arms. His tongue dipped to explore and savor her sweetness.

A crack of thunder that would have woke the dead shook the floor beneath him and brought him to his senses. The flash of brilliance accompanying the sound penetrated even his closed eyelids.

Nick ended the kiss and gently put some distance between them. And smiled.

Shelby's eyes were still closed, her lips still parted. Behind and to the right of her, LaVerne smiled blissfully. Her hands were clasped together in front of her matronly form. Without a sound, she hustled the minister and her husband from the room.

"Wow," Shelby finally said, opening her eyes lazily.

Yeah, wow, Nick thought. Shelby could definitely kiss. Every fiber of his being wanted to find out what the next level was. What else could she do so well?

"Potent stuff," she said, echoing his thoughts, then spoiled her nonchalant act by flushing to the roots of her hair. "You made the earth move."

"I wish I could take credit for it." He waved vaguely toward the window then let his hand smooth a soft curl that had escaped back into place. "Thunder."

The corner of that seductive mouth quirked and he knew he was more caught up in believing his effect on her than she was. It didn't stop him from wanting to try it again, test her reaction—and his—another time.

He gestured toward the foyer where they'd come in and followed her through the wide arched doorway. The wedding entourage was there, LaVerne with her wedding book, waiting for them to sign as Mr. and Mrs. for the first time. The two men waited with extended hands and congratulations. Then they escaped outside, into the dusky midafternoon that had grown darker.

"You promised me sun," she reminded him as they stood at the edge of the porch and looked at the sky.

A broad jog of lightning split the universe in a spectacular display. He snapped his fingers and grinned. "How about something a little flashier instead?"

"That'll do," she agreed and as if in agreement, they joined hands and made a run for it.

The sky opened the minute they stepped out from under the porch's protection, dumping rain on them in great gushes. With a gasp, Shelby waited on her side while he unlocked the little rental car.

"It has to be an omen," Shelby said breathlessly once they were firmly ensconced inside.

He couldn't think of one single thing to say. She was too far away. He drew closer, laying one arm across the back of her seat as he turned and began blotting raindrops from her upturned face with his handkerchief. Her hair had curled into ringlets. Her thin dress stuck lovingly to her in all the right places. Nick had to steel himself not to concentrate his mop-up operation there.

Her kiss-swollen lips parted and trapped his gaze as his hand slowed. He wanted to taste them again, make sure the sweetness hadn't been a figment of his imagination. Then he made the mistake of meeting her eyes. The look he found there was unconsciously inviting. Her eyes darkened with awareness and she blinked, then looked down at the fingers she'd braced against his chest. She dropped them to her lap and laced them with her other hand.

God, he wanted her.

Her chest lifted and fell in a long, silent sigh. A bone rattling boom of thunder preceded another searing bolt of lightning. And she smiled.

"What?" Nick asked, locked in his awareness of her to the point the tiniest quiver of her lip would make him wonder what was going on in her mind.

"I think we ticked him off."

Nick frowned.

"Your grandfather." She thumbed a gesture at the storm outside. "He isn't happy. You beat him, Nick."

He grinned and nodded. It was a nice image. He hoped he had made the sneaky old man mad. "Let's not count our chickens too soon. We still have tomorrow and the reading of the Will to get through." He tempered the triumph he felt.

"Let's just hope there aren't any more surprises in store," she muttered as Nick made a swipe at his own face with the hanky then started the car.

"Heat," she suggested, fiddling with the controls.

"Heat," he agreed, unsure how his skin could feel so chilled by the rain when his blood was boiling so hot beneath it.

He pulled out of the parking spot. Outside, the rain eased to a steady, rhythmic downpour that held none of the fury of a moment before.

They hadn't let the old man stay in charge too long, Nick thought. Someone had come to quell his temper tantrum. Nick thought of his father and grinned. Wouldn't it be poetic justice if his grandfather was somehow under his father's supervisory eye now? It wouldn't surprise Nick at all if his father was a top banana in the Angel Corp by now. Heaven for his dad. Hell for the old man.

What a coup! And what a fool his grandfather had been.

CHAPTER SIX

WHEN they got to the airport Don informed them they wouldn't be able to take off until the storm cell that had settled over half of Oklahoma and the southeastern part of Kansas had moved on. "I should have known," Nick muttered as the airport terminal manager said the National Weather Bureau had forecast that the storm wouldn't be out of the area for another six hours or so.

"What now?" Shelby asked as Nick sank onto the steel framed, fake leather sofa in the waiting room.

"I don't know about you," Nick said, "But I think I'm going to catch some *ZZZZs*. I'm exhausted."

"Me, too."

"I'll bet."

Her shadowed eyes took inventory of the rest of the room, the two chairs that matched the sofa, the several mismatched pieces and then back at Nick. "You gonna share that sofa with me?" she asked and he immediately felt guilty at his sprawl. He'd already lounged almost full length on it. He'd probably had more sleep in the last twenty-four hours than she had.

The word "share" had possibilities but he got up, offered it to her, then took one of the chairs.

It took him all of two minutes to realize he was tired enough to sleep in the chair but he didn't want to. Hadn't the past couple of days been stressful enough without a stiff and sore neck to add to it.

Shelby was lying on her side facing him, her head on her purse, her eyes already closed. Looking at her stirred some tender emotion he couldn't name: a combination of affection and gratitude, desire and protectiveness, pleasure and...and he was getting carried away.

Striding across the room, he crouched before her and smoothed the long hair that had fanned over her cheek back. Her eyes popped open, did a bleary impression of being just this side of oblivion, then focused. "What?"

"Asleep already?"

"If I wasn't, I was close." She batted her lush lashes at him twice, then once more for good measure.

"Let's go get a room. I saw a motel a mile or two back down the road."

Her reaction was an almost imperceptible widening of the overbright eyes.

"I don't know about you, but if I'm going to get some much-needed sleep, I'd just as soon it be comfortable and restful and—" He tilted his head toward the door of the next room where the pilots and mechanics and whatever else they were were noisily playing an intense hand of some game. "—a little quieter."

"What about...?" She waved her hand in the same general direction.

"Don?"

She nodded.

"He can come, too, if he's tired." Nick hoped he

wouldn't, though he wasn't sure why. It was only—
he checked his watch—four-thirty in the afternoon,
even though the storm and everything else had dis-
torted his sense of time. Hopefully it would only be
midnight or so when they got the all clear for takeoff.

Shelby slipped her feet into the strappy sandals
she'd kicked off and fastened them. Standing, she
braced herself with a hand on his arm, then gained
her balance and carefully lifted her hand.

She'd felt the heated rush of sensation, too, he
thought. It had marked his skin with a lingering
warmth that he was almost certain he'd be able to see
if he checked.

"Come on." He started to offer his hand but
changed his mind. It was pointless, maybe even court-
ing trouble, to encourage whatever seemed to be hap-
pening between them. He saw Shelby's knuckles
whiten as her grip tightened on her purse and knew
she was thinking the same thing. He mentally shook
the fanciful idea that he could read her mind from his
head. Shelby firmed her lips and led the way to the
adjoining room.

"Unless we don't get out of here before four tomorrow morning, I'm fine on flight time," Don assured them. "I'll stay here and keep an eye on the
weather. I can call when it clears enough that we can
take off," Don offered. He wasn't sure why he was
glad that Don didn't need sleep. He and Shelby would
get a room with a couple of beds—two rooms if
Shelby insisted—and take a good long nap. Nothing
more. But the thought of sharing Shelby, even while
they slept, didn't appeal.

The manager supplied the name of the motel they'd passed and the rental car keys that Nick had already turned in. Out of the corner of Nick's eye, he saw Shelby flush at the speculative look that passed between Don and one of the other pilots. He was fairly sure once they were out the door there would be several crude comments about honeymoons.

The rain was still coming down heavily as they made their way back to the car and left the airport. But instead of pulling into the entrance to the Thunderbird Motel, Nick turned the opposite way, into the parking lot of the discount store across the street.

"Where..."

"I thought of something we should take care of. Kind of necessary," he added at her scowl. "It'll only take a few minutes."

He started to go in without her, and was halfway to the store before he turned back reluctantly and went to open her car door. "On second thought, you'd better come with me," he said and felt an inane sense of disappointment that he wouldn't be able to surprise and impress her with his ability to think of a few of the essential details himself.

She watched curiously as he stopped inside to stare at the overhead signs indicating the various departments. He took her hand and led her toward the one marked Jewelry.

"We need wedding rings," he told the woman who came to the counter to help them.

She reached to unlock the glass display case holding diamond-encrusted sets.

"Just bands." Shelby stopped her.

"I don't mind—"

"I do," Shelby interrupted him. "I want to save at least one thrill for the real thing," she added quietly as the fortyish clerk turned to get several trays of generic wedding bands from the case behind her.

"This bothers you? You don't want to wear a ring?" Nick asked her just as quietly.

"No. You're right. We probably need them."

The woman placed the rings in front of them and discreetly moved to the other end of her little U-shaped space to assist another customer with watches. "Half of making anything believable is stage dressing and getting the details right. I assumed since you told the minister we didn't have rings and to leave that part out of the ceremony…" Her shrug finished the sentence.

"I hadn't thought of it until he asked," Nick explained as Shelby studied the rows of matching bands. She picked one up, looked at the price tag and put it back.

"You aren't even going to try it on?"

"It's almost two hundred dollars," she said, adding, "eighteen carat gold," as if that explained the price tag of the plain gold band.

Since wedding bands weren't something he'd priced, Nick was suitably impressed with the wee price. He'd expected more. He could afford the eighteen carat good stuff.

The clerk finished helping the other customer and returned. "Anything I can help you with?" she asked cheerfully.

"Which is cheapest?" Shelby wanted to know, brooking no argument when Nick started to protest that any one she wanted was fine.

"And what am I going to do with it later?" She finally met his eyes. She wasn't happy with this.

"I don't know," Nick said after a moment, "that's up to you. But it doesn't matter." She didn't want anyone to know she was his wife? He was beginning to feel as cranky as she was acting. "I can afford—"

"That's not the point." Shelby interrupted him again and put the cheapest back to ask for another. "What's the next cheapest?" she asked the saleswoman, who was keeping her mouth firmly closed as she watched the byplay between them. "That one's too big."

"You can get it—"

Shelby interrupted her, too. "We don't have time to get it sized," she told the woman and tried on the ring the clerk extended. "This one's fine," she announced and took it off so Nick could pay for it. "Aren't you going to get one?" she asked with saccharine sweetness.

He hadn't considered buying one for himself—a lot of men didn't wear wedding rings—but he wasn't about to admit it to Shelby. "Of course." He tried ones that matched hers until he found one that fit.

"I'll wait outside," Shelby told him as he got out his credit card.

"What was that about?" he asked—he thought diplomatically—as he joined Shelby under the awning outside the store. She stood, staring at the drizzle of steady rain, her arms hugged around her.

Shelby looked at him with those big green eyes, which seemed wounded somehow. Then without answering, she trudged out toward the car in the rain, her arms still locked around her midsection. He had to hurry to unlock her door so she wouldn't get more wet than she already was.

She thanked him far too politely.

"If you don't want to wear it, don't," he said tightly as he pulled across the street to the Thunderbird Motel.

She waited, staring straight ahead while he went in and got a room. His hand hovered over the register as he remembered he'd intended to ask if she'd prefer a room of her own. Damn it anyway. He wasn't going to touch her. He signed Mr. and Mrs. Nick Evans with a broad stroke of the pen and almost hoped she'd question him. He had an elaborate certificate to prove that's who she was whether she wanted anyone to know it or not.

He didn't say anything as he drove to the side wing of the building to park in front of the room they'd been assigned. She was damn lucky he hadn't asked for the bridal suite.

"Would you like to unlock the room while I lock up here?" he asked grimly. He handed her the key and reached across her to open the car door for her. His hand hesitated on the doorknob as she lifted those expressive eyes to his, then returned her gaze to the one key.

He could feel the dampness in the fabric of her

dress against his arm and could almost imagine steam rising from the heat of their bodies.

"I got two beds," he said despite his intention not to explain anything. "It's not like we're going to do anything besides nap," he added when she still hesitated. "But if you'd rather…"

"This is fine," she said in a tight voice and he opened her door to let her out into the fake stormy dusk. It was quickly fading to a real one.

He double-checked that he'd turned everything off in the unfamiliar car, then locked it and hurried in through the door she'd left open behind her. The only light she'd turned on was the one between the two beds. She sat immobile on the edge of the farthest one from the door, her shoulders raised by her stiffened arms as her fists plowed into the mattress on either side of her.

He closed the door behind him and slipped the chain into the lock. Shelby's gaze was on him as he turned, her mouth open as if she wanted to say something.

"Shelby?" He remained just inside the door.

"I'm sorry," she finally said. "I don't know what's wrong with me."

He made his way across to her, jamming his hands into his pockets to keep from reaching for her. He took them out when he sank on the bed opposite her, imitating her posture. "You don't have to wear the ring if you don't want to," he reiterated.

"It's not…I don't know what's wrong with me," she added with a quiet moan. She swiped a finger beneath one of her downcast eyes.

"Shelby." Every bit of his concern was in his voice. "Are you crying?"

"Yes," she said, her voice breaking in a mix somewhere between one of her melodious laughs and a sob. "And I don't even know why." She swung her legs up to the bed and leaned back against the headboard.

He tilted the yellowed shade of the lamp up so he could see her face and she reached to tip it down again. "I'm being ridiculous. Ignore me."

"Can you at least give me a hint." He was fiercely determined to do something about whatever it was. He had to fight himself to keep from taking her in his arms, but knew with some inner certainty that would make it worse. Whatever the problem, he was part of it.

"The ring just suddenly made it real," she half whispered.

"And you're having regrets?"

"Yes. No." She sniffed once and laughed self-deprecatingly again, wiping at the same eye she'd dabbed before with her knuckle. "I knew what I was doing. I want to do it," she added as if she was arguing with herself. "I want to help you. I want your mother to have everything she should. It's not that. It's just..." She cleared her throat and turned so he could see her in the light. All trace of the tears were gone from her eyes. They were just overly bright. "A wedding day is supposed to be so joyous," she finished softly. "And...and..."

"And?" He waited.

"Buying rings at Walmart in the rain seemed to...to..."

"Emphasize that everything is wrong." He finished the sentence for her.

She nodded. "See. I told you it was silly."

The tears were completely gone. The rush of...of...something he felt for her almost overwhelmed him. Gratitude. The rush of feeling was gratitude. And he wanted desperately to show it. The only thing that came to mind had nothing to do with gratitude. But he *could* take care of her, he realized and stood to turn and sit himself down on the edge of her bed.

Her eyes widened as she looked up at him. He glanced quickly away.

"Well, I probably can't make this all joyous," he said, "but I can make you comfortable. See that you get some rest. That'll make everything a hundred times better," he promised. "You're tired. That's part of this. And I've asked a lot of you."

He unfastened the buckles on her sandals as he spoke and tried not to think of her shapely legs as he let the shoes fall one by one to the floor. "And I can—" he reached across and tugged the bedspread off his bed "—find you something warm to wrap up in so we can get that dress on a hanger to dry out a little." He draped the bedspread across her shoulders, carefully avoiding her eyes. He could *feel* her warm pleasure in the way she was looking at him and he refused to be responsible for his body's reaction to it. "You get comfortable. I'll...go in the bathroom and wash my face or something. And don't worry about the dress," he ordered. "I'll hang it up for you."

Nick stared in the bathroom mirror, splashed cold water on his face and considered taking a cold shower. Talk about a way to complicate things! The thoughts and urges and feelings he was having were next to insane. He propped his hands on the edge of the counter and studied his physical similarities to his grandfather. *That* should get his head on straight. The purpose of this whole thing was to beat his grandfather at his last attempt at playing a foolish game. "Without hurting anyone else or messing up their lives," he muttered. Including his or Shelby's.

"It's okay, Nick," he heard her call as if thinking her name brought some mystical, magical response from her.

Burying his face in a towel, he dried then slung it around his shoulders.

Shelby had wrapped herself Indian style in the bedspread he'd given her and lay on her side, facing the other bed. Her golden brown hair flowed over the white pillowcase in a tangled disarray.

His fingers itched to smooth it and he clenched his jaw as if he thought that would help. The light from the lamp haloed her in a protective, warm circle.

"Thanks," he heard her murmur groggily as he picked up her dress from the end of her bed. He quietly hung it on a hanger on the rack near the bathroom.

"I just hope it gets dry," he offered, as much for something to say as anything. "You won't mind if I take off my shirt?'' he asked, tugging the hem from his pants.

"Of course not. I'll bet it's damp, too," she added. Her voice caressed him, sending a pleasant sensation rippling up and down his spine. Except where his muscles were stiff. Tension, he explained the tightness as he wandered to the small nightstand between the beds to remove the accumulated change and his billfold from his pants pockets.

Shelby was looking at him when he looked down at her.

"Can I ask you something?"

"Sure." He settled again on the side of his bed and slipped off his shoes.

She pulled his bedspread tighter around her neck as he wondered what she had on beneath it now.

"What is it you have against marriage, Nick?" she asked.

He grimaced and lifted one shoulder. "Nothing, really."

Her lids drooped sleepily as she grinned, half of it hidden by her pillow. "Sure. You've sounded like you're gung ho about the subject all day."

"I didn't plan to do it myself," he admitted. "But I don't have anything against it for anyone else."

"Oh." She nestled further into her cocoon. "But you have no specific reason why?"

"Marriage has always seemed to be about what you're willing to give up." He rubbed his tired shoulder.

"I guess I don't know what you mean," she said after a minute. He'd thought she'd fallen asleep.

"Well, you *know* what my mother gave up," he said pointedly.

She nodded as well as she could, given her position. "And what did your father give up? Other women?"

The warm affection he always felt thinking of Nicholas Evans, Sr. came through in his chuckle. "That is one thing women seem to expect you to give up when you get married," he teased Shelby. "But no, for some reason, that didn't seem to bother him. No," he went on, "you know the plane we flew in today?"

She nodded again.

"Dad always dreamed of having one something like that. He never could afford it 'cause he was raising a family. Then when he was getting to the place he might have been able to have it..."

"He died," she finished when he didn't. "Before he could realize his dreams."

"Yeah, he died," Nick agreed and would have risen.

"So things are more important to you than marriage," she said before he could.

"Not things so much," he contradicted, because she made it sound a lot more selfish and self-centered than he felt it. "But dreams are important, don't you think?" Shelby had her own dreams.

She'd made it clear that she took steps to achieve them every chance she got.

"Uh-huh," she agreed.

"My dad was a pilot when he met Mom. He wanted to fly commercially. He gave that up because Mom hated the thought of him traveling all the time.

She thought the life-style wouldn't be very conducive to having a good marriage.''

"And he was unhappy?"

"Not in the least, I don't think," Nick admitted. "He seemed really content with his life."

"But you feel he was slighted in some way."

He had to think on that question for a moment. "I think what he did was okay for him—he was happy with it—but it isn't something I would choose."

"What dream do you have that you think some woman might want you to give up," she asked, her tone becoming softer and less definitive with each word.

"My prime examples are all past tense," he said dryly, rising to finish taking off his shirt.

"Oh?"

"One woman I'd only been out with a couple of times actually hinted if we continued I'd have to get rid of my car."

"Ah. She didn't trust you. She thought it was blonde bait?" He heard the grin in Shelby's voice.

"Or that it wasn't a suitable car for a family," he said, unbuttoning buttons. "The biggest ultimatum was from a woman in college." The one woman he'd asked to marry him, he didn't add.

"What'd she want you to give up? Biology?" she teased softly.

"She wanted me to give up my plans to go into teaching," he said. "Her family had some kind of business that she wanted me to go into."

"That one does sound a little more seri—my God, Nick, what happened?"

Before Nick could react to the dismay in Shelby's voice, she jumped from the bed, brushed past him and crossed to the door to flip on the more illuminating light over the dresser. He had his shirt off with the intent of going to hang it beside her dress. She stopped him, gently grazing his shoulder with the fingertip of one hand while she clasped her wrap around her shoulders with the other. Her touch sent shivers down his spine.

He braced himself not to flinch, carefully cupped her hand in his and pulled it away from him, then glanced in the mirror behind Shelby.

He whistled and stepped closer. One heck of a blue-black bruise decorated his shoulder.

The purse snatcher, he remembered. The jerk had kicked him trying to escape. Damn, he wished he'd caught him. "It must have happened this morning."

She moved closer, concern turning the edges of her mouth down. Her fingers brushed the spot again. He caught them and turned back to her, away from their reflections in the mirror. No matter how much logic he applied, he no longer had the desire nor the energy to fight off his impulses if she touched him that way.

"I didn't know you were hurt."

Her voice was as hard to resist as her hands. "I didn't realize either till just now," he said, "so I must not have been hurt too badly."

Her wide compassionate gaze steadied on his face. "It doesn't hurt now?" She disengaged her hand from the clamp he had on it.

"I've been getting slower and slower all day," he admitted absently. "I thought it was tension and stress." They were standing close, their gazes had locked. The only way he could tear his gaze away was to lower it to her mouth.

Her hand came back to his shoulder, but this time she didn't look at the marred skin she had skimmed her fingers over. Her gaze held tight on his and he almost didn't notice that her blanket had slid to a heap around her feet. That she was in a longish, lacy slip registered somewhere in his mind.

Her fingers combed through his hair in an attempt to push away the lock of hair that constantly fell over his forehead.

His hand went automatically to a wavy strand of her hair at the corner of her brow. She froze, her arm still raised, her hand still in his hair. "We're playing with fire here, aren't we?" The words came in a breathless rush.

He nodded, or at least meant to, he wasn't sure if he did or not as he waited expectantly for her to pull away. When she didn't, he gave in to the urge to explore the soft, silky skin just beneath the tiny curl. Every movement seemed like slow motion. Her arm dropped to her side. The tip of her tongue sneaked out to dampen the graceful bow of her mouth, then quickly hid again so she could gnaw at her lower lip with her straight white teeth.

She gasped as his fingers gently cupped her neck. "I'm sorry you were hurt—" her breath became wispy again as he stroked the translucent skin from her hairline to her collarbone "—for...me." Her fingers fluttered against his shoulder then moved away.

The air seemed charged with something ready to ignite.

He wanted that spark, that something that would set them ablaze. He was going to kiss her. He knew without a doubt he was going to kiss her. The worst she could do was hit him. Or get mad. Or... something. And the something might be bliss.

He dipped his head, hesitated, waiting for her to back away. Instead she lifted her lips ever so slightly toward his.

The contact of his mouth against hers stirred something in his soul. It was delicate, shimmery, intangible. Her response was mind numbing and left him wanting more. She braced her hand lightly against his chest then let it fall away. But her lips lingered and held.

He had to come up for air.

But he couldn't resist the warmth of her lips for more than a second.

"Shelby." Her name felt like liquid heat on his tongue and sounded even better against her lips. His arms engulfed her, drawing her closer to his chest. The brush of her silky slip against his bare chest turned want to need.

Her weak "This is crazy" told him she wasn't quite as mesmerized and mindless as he hoped.

"I know," he agreed and kissed her again, giving in to the hungry need to feel the length of her against him. He pulled her closer.

She settled her hands against his chest, between them, but still didn't push him away as he expected. He let his hand explore the length of her back as her fingers slid slowly up to his neck. Her touch was magic. He tightened his embrace. With her hand out of the way, he could feel her exquisite breasts flatten against him. "What are we doing here, Shelby?"

His palms ached to explore them.

"I don't know. Oh, Nick." He tucked an experimental kiss on the pulse point beneath her ear, anticipating a slow exploration downward toward the satin mounds of flesh rising above the double layer of lace only inches away.

And finally, she pushed herself away. "You're really good at that," she said shakily.

All sorts of things swelled with pleasure at her words. Her face was slightly flushed. Her eyes glimmered.

"You could give lessons yourself," he echoed her approval.

She laughed huskily and her face turned bright pink. "It was a kiss." From the tilt of her upturned nose, he could tell she meant to say it nonchalantly, but the words escaped in a breathless whisper. "Just a kiss." That managed to sound a little more normal. "It's been that kind of day. You know?" She spread her hands, backing away. "I...I think we are both so tired and strung out that we no longer have any idea what we're doing."

He knew exactly what he was doing. And exactly what he wanted to do. "We do have the license."

"That's almost the best line I've ever heard." Her husky chuckle was forced and not nearly as blasé as she was trying for. "Which isn't surprising, considering you're the only one who could legitimately use it." She concentrated on picking up the bedspread from around her feet and rewrapping herself in it.

"We are married." He felt obligated to drive the point home. He suspected she was feeling weak.

She tossed her head. "And I've never told a single man I was waiting for a marriage license."

"I'm not single," he quipped.

She laughed and this time, it was full of genuine pleasure.

He felt witty and wonderful and suddenly serious. "*Are* you waiting for something?"

"Love." The soft flush that was so appealing painted Shelby's face but her gaze held steady. "I've always waited for love." She sighed, then wrapped her blanket tighter around her and made her way back to the bed. "Now. I'm going to get some sleep so I might be halfway sane tomorrow."

Tomorrow. He hadn't thought of his mother or the funeral or tomorrow in what seemed like forever. "I have to call Mom," he said as much to himself as to her and was thankful to have something to take his mind off the seductive waif who laid her head down on the pillow in the bed he'd like to join her in.

By the time he got the number his mother had left on his answering machine, Nick could hear Shelby softly snoring. "Mrs. Evans is at the visitation for her father," the dignified voice that answered the phone told him.

"Can I leave a message?" Nick asked.

"Certainly, sir."

After making it clear that he didn't expect her to meet his plane, Nick left the flight number he and

Shelby would be on in the morning and hung up. Then he called Don at the terminal and suggested he let them sleep most of the night, even if the weather cleared—unless the forecast predicted that it would get nasty again.

"Tomorrow's supposed to be sunny and clear," Don told him and agreed that since they already had a room, it would be pointless to rush back to Kansas City much before their flight to St. Louis. They arranged a takeoff time and rang off.

Nick set the alarm clock then wandered outside to watch the storm and breathe in the cool air. Without his shoes or shirt, the spray and splatter from the rain-drenched wind was almost as good as a cold shower. The effect wore off the minute he glanced back through the open door at Shelby.

Not exactly a wedding night to tell your grandkids about.

The thought brought a wry smile. Hey. There was a bright side to everything. At least he could say now he'd had a wedding night. It wasn't something he'd expected to experience. The thought that there wouldn't be any grandkids to tell it to made him frown.

CHAPTER SEVEN

THE rain had stopped by three-thirty the next morning. It was perfect weather for flying.

"Do you regularly get up at this time of day?" Shelby asked irritably as they let themselves out of the room.

The realization that he'd known her a little less than twenty-four hours hit him like a thunderbolt and he'd been up both mornings before his usual six. He unlocked her side of the car. "The only time I can remember *seeing* this time of day from this side are the days I've been married," he said lightly.

"That's an argument for divorce if I ever heard one," she muttered then said a few indelicate words as she burned her mouth on the too hot coffee he'd brought them from a twenty-four-hour convenience store while she was taking a quick shower.

She was the only woman he'd ever met who was cute even when she was irritable. She wasn't exactly Miss Merry Sunshine when she first woke up. Or maybe it was the time. She hadn't exactly been joyous at this hour yesterday, either, and she hadn't been to bed yet. Then he remembered what she'd been doing when he met her.

"Your dog," he exclaimed. "Is someone taking care of it? When I asked Don to let us sleep straight

115

through, I didn't figure in time for us to run home. We're going to need to go straight to the airport.''

For a moment, she looked blank. "Oh, the dog food. That was for my neighbor.''

"One of your jobs?'' He pulled the car into the small Miami airport.

"If it was a job, I wouldn't have been doing it then,'' she said dryly. "My neighbor and I share a duplex and sort of share Oscar—her dog,'' she added. "He guards my place, too, barking like crazy when anyone comes. He's my buddy. He likes me.''

Her first happy thought of the day. Nick liked her, too, he had to admit. Even grouchy. "Maybe he likes you because you buy his dog food?'' he suggested tongue-in-cheek since talking about Oscar seemed to mellow her.

She sniffed at him. "Martha's elderly, doesn't get out much.'' She took a noisy sip of hot coffee. "I knew Oscar'd need dog food this morning. Yesterday morning.'' She corrected herself then looked too confused to care. "I didn't want to get up early so I stopped at the grocery store to pick some up on my way home from the anniversary thingy.''

She made him smile again and he thought some man would be happy to get her someday. She'd definitely keep him amused.

"First mistake.'' She lifted a finger, talking to herself again.

"What? The anniversary party? Stopping at the grocery store on your way home? Or running into me?''

VAL DANIELS 117

"Being out this time of day to begin with," she mumbled. "What are you smiling about?"

"Sorry." He turned off the ignition but couldn't seem to turn off the smile. "You're an easy touch, aren't you?"

"Whatever gave you the first clue?"

He reached across the space between them and smoothed the furrow she'd creased into her brow.

She flinched away. Her gleaming eyes met his in a stray beam of light from the building.

"An easy touch—" he bent to angle an appreciative kiss on the corner of her grimly set mouth "—and touchy, too."

"Thank you," she said dryly.

"You're welcome."

She ducked, avoiding his eyes, and busily groped for her purse. Her hand came up with the small plastic bag from the discount store they'd left in the car last night. She dropped it like a hot potato. "You don't want to put this on now, I take it?" He picked it up.

Her hand clenched automatically.

"You don't have to." He took the rings from the sack. They clanked together in his palm as he stretched to put them in the pocket of his slacks.

"Oh, okay." She spread her fingers wide and extended her hand.

He slipped her wedding band into place. "See, that didn't hurt a bit." Satisfaction settled in his chest.

"Oh, yes it did," she disagreed and picked the other ring from his palm. Grabbing his hand, she jammed it home on his finger. "If I have to wear one, you do, too. You need the receipt?" she asked.

He shook his head.

She crumpled the empty bag. Grabbing the coffee cup she'd set on the floor, she let herself out and was halfway to the building before Nick got the car locked and followed.

"How does it hurt?" he called, his low voice echoing loudly against the metal encased building and back at him.

"It's a walking, talking lie." The ring on the hand she held up over her shoulder glimmered wickedly in the light a second before she disappeared into the building. "How am I going to find a *real* husband wearing this?"

A *real* husband? He ground his teeth and wondered if he'd just been insulted.

The flight to Kansas City was quiet and uneventful. If it took time for Shelby to become civil after she awoke, he decided, it was safest not to talk to her.

He loved flying in the middle of the night. The stars were close and bright, almost as bright as Shelby's sleep dazed eyes.

Nick could think of worse things than stargazing with her...if he was the stargazing type. And if she was in a better mood. She leaned against the far side of the plane, staring straight ahead at the night sky and ignoring him.

He leaned forward and talked to Don instead. They talked about the flight lessons his father had given him for his seventeenth birthday, about his renewed interest and about Don's experiences as a charter operator.

By the time they landed at the downtown airport, Nick knew he was going to start lessons again.

It was five-thirty in the morning with an hour and a half to spare before their scheduled flight to St. Louis. Shelby insisted on getting her suitcase out of the car and changing before they drove to KCI.

Nick carried her suitcase into the big brick building that served as the downtown terminal. "I should have taken our bags with us to Miami," he told her.

"You didn't know it was going to storm," she said evenly, evidence that her good temper was almost restored sneaking through in a grin. "Don said we should make it back by eight-thirty or nine last night. If you'd suggested taking our bags, I'd have thought you were going to try and come up with some lame excuse to get me alone on our wedding night."

"Worked, didn't it?" They were outside the women's rest room. He handed her the garment bag.

"Even you don't have that much pull," she said, tossing her hair at him as she disappeared inside.

She reappeared wearing another longish white dress that looked like someone had spilled a wild bouquet of lilacs on it. She stopped in front of him. "Will this be okay, do you think? It isn't very sad looking but it does look springish. I only have—"

"It's very pretty, Shelby." He interrupted her quietly. To heck with looking like you were in mourning when you didn't even know the deceased. It wasn't as though she'd had time to prepare for this funeral. For once, she wasn't perfect for the occasion.

But she took Nick's breath away. The lilac bouquet hugged her body down past her waist to where her hips flared. The piping around the lowered waist came to a point in the center of the full skirt. A wide collar spanned her shoulders, lying low, leaving them bare. The wealth of skin showing gave only a hint of the slope of her breasts and the collar teasingly emphasized while hiding her generous curves. "Perfect."

"I didn't want to meet your mother in that black thing," she said, destroying his delusion that she was going to be less than perfect as they got in the car for the drive to the other airport. "I will have time to change before the funeral, don't you think?"

The perfect size stapler to fix a hanging button; the perfect run-away-to-get-married "wedding" dress; the perfect meet-your-mother-in-law dress; he had no doubt the 'black thing' in her suitcase would be the perfect funeral garb. She'd be the perfect wife. And she scared him to death.

"Hey, I still have pants to hem," he reminded her and promised, "We'll make time."

"We ought to be coming up with our story," she suggested after a moment. "What are we going to tell your mom?" The rest of the trip to the airport and while they waited for their flight to be called, they made plans and compared notes for the "next phase."

They were quiet on the flight, each lost in their own thoughts.

"I hate this," Shelby murmured as the flight attendant prepared for landing.

"What?"

"Funerals. Pretending to be something I'm not. Lying. Being married," she said. "Take your choice."

"I thought you wanted to be married." He decided he'd found something about her that wasn't perfect. Her irritable mood.

"Not like this," she denied. "The sooner we're done with this, the better."

The plane was descending and Nick couldn't tell if the tricks his stomach was doing were a result of that or Shelby's words. The jolt as they touched down matched the jolt to his ego. It shouldn't bother him that she wanted this to be over as badly as he did, but it did.

"Shelby, it's not too late if you don't want to go through with this part. You've done what I really needed. I have the legal document." He leaned up to pat his billfold where he'd placed the folded marriage certificate. "I can get you a ticket on the next flight ho—"

"Ignore me," she said, rubbing her temples. "You'll get your money's worth," she added.

"I already have my money's worth." He realized he believed every word. "The rest is icing."

"I just want to do this right," she said, unfastening her seat belt. "I'm not sure…"

"I am." He linked his hand with hers for a minute. "I am," he said again. The crowd around them was gathering their things to disembark. He stood and got their bags from the overhead compartment. He stepped aside for her to precede him.

She smoothed the generous skirt around her, shaping it to her body. Her hand shook, almost imperceptibly, but it did shake. She did the best I-can-take-anything-you-can-throw-at-me imitation he'd ever seen, he realized with a rush of protectiveness.

But she wasn't quite as assured and confident as she acted, he realized with a sense of pleasure that bewildered him. She just struggled to be. Anyone who tried as hard as Shelby did to do the "right thing" deserved some help along the way.

He'd give her all he had.

They were at the rental counter to pick up the car Nick had arranged for when a older man in a black suit approached them.

"Nicholas Evans?" the man asked tentatively.

Nick straightened and Shelby stepped closer. Nick wasn't sure if she was seeking protection or offering it. He couldn't help his inward smile. He felt protected.

The man stuck out his hand. "I'm Bradley Vaughn. Your grandfather's attorney?"

Nick accepted the guy's hand. "You won't be needing a car," he said. "I have one waiting."

"How'd you know which flight we'd be on?" Nick asked warily.

"Your mother sent me."

"So she did get my message?"

"Of course." The man started to leave, expecting them to follow.

Nick looked at Shelby. *Do we want to be at this man's mercy?*

She obviously had her mental telepathy receiver on. "It might be nice to have a car," she suggested as Mr. Vaughn turned back to see what was keeping them. It didn't escape Nick that the less time they spent with other people, the less time they'd have to fake anything.

The woman behind the counter informed him a day's rental had been charged to his card when he made the reservation, sealing the decision.

"We're going to take the car," he told the lawyer as he rejoined them. "I have to pay for it anyway." He held up the keys. He trusted his grandfather's lawyer about as much as he'd trust the old man himself. Did he want any of them to be at the mercy of a proven control freak's sidekick, stranded wherever his grandfather's lawyer decided to strand them?

"I'll drop you by the lot." Mr. Vaughn offered, directing a frankly curious look at Shelby since Nick hadn't yet introduced them.

Nick watched him carefully. "Mr. Vaughn," he said, "my wife, Shelby."

She turned into a stars-in-her-eyes bride right before Nick's eyes.

The man recovered from his shock almost instantly. It would have escaped unnoticed had Nick not been expecting it. Vaughn said all the right things, ending with a "Follow me."

"Where are we going?"

"Your grandfather's house," the attorney said. "I'm sure you'll want to relax, have a bite to eat—" his expansive gesture seemed to add anything of their choosing to the list "—before the funeral this afternoon."

"My mother's there?" He'd been going to call his answering machine after they picked up the car to see if she'd left another message telling them where to meet her.

Mr. Vaughn assured them she'd be waiting at the house.

The car they rode to the rental lot in was a limo. The house he and Shelby followed Mr. Vaughn and his driver to was a mansion. For the first time in his life, Nick understood his father's oft proudly quoted, sometimes regretful "You don't know what she gave up for me."

No. He hadn't known. He still thought his mother had gotten the best end of the deal.

Shelby whistled under her breath as Nick pulled the little car up behind the limo. "Your mama loved your daddy a *lot*," she said in a down-home accent.

A lot, he thought, nodding numbly.

The monstrosity the lawyer had called a house had three stories, possibly four. Nick squinted trying to tell if the dormers on the sharply pitched roof were real or there for show. For show, he was almost certain though it might be attic space.

The yard—or should he say grounds? The meticulously cared for lawn covered at least five acres just in the front—was surrounded by a twelve foot, foot and a half thick solid brick fence. The gates they'd just driven through were made of stately looking wrought iron and trimmed in brass.

Mr. Vaughn hopped out of the limo spryly and headed toward the house where Nick saw his mother waiting at the open front door. Both inside and out, people milled around. Cars were strung the length of the circular driveway with more arriving at steady intervals. People dressed in appropriate funeral attire were making their way to the house.

He'd thought he'd at least have time to introduce his new wife to his mother without an audience.

Shelby must have been thinking the same thing. "For some reason, I thought this would be a little more private." Although she didn't sound as if she liked it, she seemed to have her nerves firmly under control now.

Nick unfolded slowly from the car, still trying to get the kinks out after two cramped flights and the small car. Shelby let herself out the other side.

"What do you think?" Marsha called, hurrying toward him with both hands outstretched. She looked around, walking backward a couple of steps, and narrowed her eyes as if she wanted to see it through his. "Some place, huh?"

"Some place," he agreed. "This is the house you grew up in, Mom?"

Marsha nodded, still staring at it. "I haven't forgotten an inch of it."

He realized now, away from the crowd, might be the best time to break his news. He extended a hand to Shelby who had followed him to the front of the car. "My turn to ask what you think." He pulled Shelby to him, encircling her waist with his arm as his mother became aware for the first time that he'd brought someone with him. "I'd like you to meet someone very special, Mom. This is Shelby—" he paused only a second before he added "—my wife."

In the process of extending her hand to Shelby, his mother left it hanging in midair as she gasped and did a double take. For a minute, Nick thought she was going to faint at his feet. He prepared to catch her.

"Shelby. My mother, Marsha Evans."

The questions filling Marsha's eyes didn't make it past her lips. Her mouth still hung open in silence. Her face went through an exhibition of all her expressions in seconds.

Shelby closed the distance between his mother's hand and her own. "I'm delighted to meet you, Mrs. Evans," she said, then looked back at Nick expectantly, willing him with her eyes to take over again.

Nick said softly, "Mom? You okay?"

She finally found her tongue. "How? Wha...?"

"Life's short, Mom. Nothing's made that clearer than the past couple of days." The line he'd rehearsed and ran past Shelby this morning fell easily from his lips. "Grandfather's death." He gently touched her cheek. "What you said the other night about wishing things could have been different. Shelby's run-in with a mugger...my little accident yesterday morning..." He lifted a shoulder. "I decided I didn't want to be alone anymore. I didn't want to go anywhere without Shelby again." As if on cue, Shelby wrapped her arm around his waist and looked up at him adoringly. She was starting to get into the loving wife routine. "When I couldn't make the flight yesterday, we used the time wisely. We eloped."

"Oh, Shelby..." Shelby was on the receiving end of a hug. "Nick..." Flabbergasted and overwhelmed, she didn't know what to say or do. She threw herself at both of them. "How did you do this?" she asked Shelby. "The confirmed bachelor finally gets his comeuppance,'' she directed at him without giving either of them a chance to respond. "I didn't think he'd ever marry. Now I can hope for grandkids." Before she finished the statement it turned into a fishing expedition, her voice rising at the end.

"Don't hold your breath, Mom. We aren't in a big hurry." *Shelby's not pregnant if that's what you're asking,* he wanted to say.

She looked almost disappointed. "Your father would be so ecstatic, Nick." Her eyes filled with sentimental tears. "We were never quite sure what we did to put you off marriage. I just knew he'd fall hard...*if* he ever fell," she whispered with conviction to Shelby. She started herding them toward the house but stopped before they'd taken two steps. "What accident? You never did tell me what happened. What—"

"It's too long and involved, Mom. I promise, we'll give you all the details later," he added when she would have asked another question.

"I can hardly wait to announce to everyone—"

"Mom." He did manage to curtail her this time. "Please, can we wait? We don't know these people. It's not their business when or how long we've been married. This isn't exactly a celebratory occasion. Can Shelby and I enjoy our happiness—peacefully and in private?"

She looked at them uncertainly.

"Please," Shelby said, "I felt funny about this anyway. Rushing to get married right before a funeral. There are people who will think it's inappropriate.

And that's not what we wanted at all. We saw it as...as...a..." She let the statement trail.

"A reaffirmation of life?" Marsha picked up on the thought, just as Shelby obviously hoped she would. Her eyes filled with tears once more and Nick gave Shelby points for coming through with just the right touch yet again. "Oh, it is, Shelby. It's the perfect affirmation of life."

Nick had expected to find her ensconced in a room at a hotel near the funeral home, not in the midst of a mob scene at a mansion. "Who are all these people anyway?"

"Friends."

Nick bit his tongue as the word vultures sprang to his mind. A controlling, domineering old man like the one he'd met on the videotape wouldn't have many friends.

"Employees," his mother went on. "Members of the Board of Directors of Celidon."

"Celidon?" Shelby had mostly been quiet. "The catalog place?"

Marsha nodded, obviously pleased that her new daughter-in-law knew the company name. "You know it?"

"I probably paid for this house," Shelby exaggerated. "I think my whole apartment is decorated in stuff from Celidon. I love their catalogs."

"Why are they all here?" Nick asked, returning to his original question.

"A dinner for family and friends. It's a buffet. Some of it's catered. The rest has been taken care of by the staff."

"Don't they usually do this after the funeral—for family and close friends?" Nick added.

"Sometimes. Mr. Vaughn made the arrangements according to Dad's instructions. Those who've been invited to return after the funeral will be here for the reading of his Will."

She turned in front of them. "I think, oh Nick, it looks like…" She stumbled over the words, flustered. "Oh, Nick, I think I'm going to inherit this."

He and Shelby exchanged looks over the top of her head. "Everything, Mom?"

"I don't know," she admitted. "The house at least. Mr. Vaughn met my plane and brought me here. Everyone—the household staff, the members of the board of directors—treats me like I'm in charge now."

"That's what you want?" He didn't really need to ask. Her face confirmed that he'd made the right choice in marrying Shelby.

She nodded and a tear wobbled at the edge of her eye. "I guess he loved me after all."

"Too little, too late." He tried to keep the sneer he felt out of his voice.

"He was just stubborn," she said, excusing the man who'd fathered her. "Like other people I know," she added, eyeing him and then extending a warning glance to Shelby that seemed to say she knew exactly where Nick got his stubborn streak. "Whatever my father did or didn't have, he did have a sense a humor. I promise you, whatever he decided to do, it will be interesting."

The look Shelby sent him said she wholeheartedly

agreed with his thought that "interesting" might not be a graphic enough word.

Marsha led them around the main part of the house and introduced them to a few of the people present. After she escorted them to the buffet set up at long side tables in a great dining room, she turned their care over to a man she introduced as Michael.

When they'd eaten, he showed them more of the house then led them to a room upstairs. Indicating that their luggage had been brought and unpacked, he showed them where their things were. "The suit and black dress are being pressed. We took the liberty of assuming that was what you'd want prepared for the funeral," he added when Nick expressed concern that his new suit bag wasn't hanging in the huge empty closet with Shelby's things.

"We have to hem them," Shelby remembered and started rummaging through her purse for the tape.

"I'll do it." In her continual effort to do and be everything for everybody, it would be very easy to take Shelby for granted. Or get used to depending on her.

"It won't be necessary for either of you," Michael assured them. "The hem is marked?"

"They marked it at the store," Shelby said.

"Then Beverly will notice," Michael said. "I'm sure she's hemmed the pants already, but I'll double-check, just to be safe," he added when Shelby would have said something else. "Is there anything else I can get you?"

Just anxious for him to leave, Nick shook his head.

"I'm sure everything's fine," Shelby said. "More than fine," she murmured, looking around the room as the door closed behind him.

They stared at each other, holding their breath, waiting for Michael's footsteps to recede down the hall.

"That went well, don't you think?" Shelby whispered. Gone were the stars in her eyes, the tender voice, the indulgent looks she'd displayed for his mother.

Thank heavens she was half a room away and keeping her hands to herself. Her wifely act and constant possessive touches since they'd arrived made it difficult to remember they weren't a loving couple. "What'd you do? Practice before you came?"

"I was in a lot of plays in high school." She proudly lifted her chin at his implied approval.

"You're good," he said. "You dazzled even me," he added, more honestly than she knew. But that had nothing to do with her acting ability. Her very proximity was enough to make his heart race like he'd just ran a mile.

She shrugged. "Thanks. Nice room. I suppose I could get used to this luxury." She poked the mattress with a casual air that didn't ring true. Her act wasn't nearly as good in private.

His mother had put them on the second floor in the nicest room of four in this wing. It was bigger than the bedroom in the master suite Marsha had proudly shown them. But instead of her small, separate sitting room, this room had a large bow window at one end, which held a desk with a chair and a chaise longue. They also had an attached bath and a huge closet.

"You're comfortable with this arrangement then?" he asked, copying her nonchalance. They'd planned to get adjoining rooms in whatever hotel Marsha was in. They'd put everything in one room, but Nick would sleep in the other, easily accessible should he be needed. Now here they were, one room, one bed. And no way they could change it without creating questions neither of them wanted to answer.

"Comfortable isn't the right word." She became absorbed in studying the room. "But I can handle it if you can. Hey, we got lucky," she said a shade too cheerfully, "it's a king-size bed. We don't even have to touch each other."

Nick suppressed a groan. It had nothing to do with whether he touched her or not. He wished with all his heart it was that easy. It was the *wanting* to touch her that would make him nuts. And with the enforced closeness of the past couple of hours and the memory of her kiss last night, he wanted to do a lot more than touch.

"Your mother will expect us to sleep together."

"If I sneak next door—"

"We might get by with that if there weren't a whole raft of servants all over the place."

"I can sleep on top of the covers. Not even unmake the bed. If I set my alarm, I could be back in here before anyone else is up."

"Oh? And how do you know what time people get up around here?" She shook her head in disbelief.

"Or for that matter, who else will be staying in this huge house tonight."

"I know." He agreed, irritated at himself for feeling as if he might go up in flames just watching her stand on the other side of the room.

"We can handle anything for another twenty-four hours," she assured him determinedly.

She laced her fingers together and started laying out more plans. By the time Michael brought their clothes back they'd worked out a specific way to cope with the unexpected arrangement. Nick dressed in the closet while she took a turn in front of the bathroom mirror. Then they switched.

"See? This isn't so bad, is it?" Shelby asked as they crossed paths. Her lightweight robe covered as much as anything he'd seen her in, but his mouth began to water, thinking of what she might not have on underneath. "Probably better than the motel yesterday," she added as she shut the door between them again.

And that was part of the problem. Last night, added to the early morning, added to the day so far, added to an endless prospect of having her close and sensuous and smelling good and looking better and knowing all the right things to do or say and how to handle every situation they faced. She brought out every tender, proud, fascinated, frustrated, crazy, obsessed feeling he'd ever had. If he wasn't careful, he'd begin to think the smartest thing he'd ever done was marry her.

And except for the brief aberration this morning when she'd let her "perfect" mask slip, she seemed to be the one keeping reality in view. She was coping and planning and acting exactly as she should, while never losing sight that it was all a temporary job. She could handle anything for another twenty-four hours, huh?

Ms. Perfect was beginning to annoy the hell out of him.

CHAPTER EIGHT

NICK expected a small memorial service in an impersonal mortuary chapel. It was an extravagant event in a plush uptown cathedral. It played to a packed house of the crème de la crème of St. Louis society.

Although there were tissues and hankies aplenty in evidence, the only person Nick saw using one was his mom—and Shelby. He sat between them, cradling Shelby's hand, his arm around his mother, holding her close to his chest. He ended with the positions reversed. His mother sat stoically, dabbing at tears from time to time while they coursed down Shelby's cheeks and she seemed to fold gradually inward and toward him. Comforting Shelby kept his mind off the only emotion he could seem to bring forth for the man they were supposed to be mourning: a cold disdain.

As the elaborate graveside service finished a little later, they stepped back and away as his mother began to accept a steady stream of condolences. Shelby looked up at him, her normally clear eyes red-rimmed and puffy.

"I hope I'm not embarrassing you."

"No." Holding her eased the guilt he felt for feeling nothing. "But I'm not sure why you're upset," he added. "You didn't even know him."

"That's the sad thing." She sniffed and pressed her tissue to her eye. "He didn't know *you*. And your

135

mother..." Her hand waved vaguely in that direction as big tears welled again in her eyes. "The way they were. It's so sad."

She brought a lump to his throat, but it wasn't with thoughts of Chester Celinski. Shelby's capacity for tenderness made him ache inside.

"I've embarrassed me." She half giggled nervously. "But I cry over everything. Weddings. Funerals. Telephone company commercials. And when anyone else cries..." She drew away from him, blew her nose. "I almost feel it's my duty." She rested her forehead against his chest, hiding her eyes, he suspected. He wrapped his arms around her and held her tight. Something about it gave him peace.

His mother finally joined them. Shelby stood aside, widening the circle and inviting Marsha to share Nick's embrace.

"How are you doing?" He could only see the top of her head.

She looked up at him as if cooperating. "I'm fine."

Her face was pale and pinched. Her eyes were a mild shade of pink. For the first time he could remember, his mother looked her age.

"I'd say as well as could be expected would be more accurate," he said gently.

"But I needed this. I needed to tell him goodbye." His mother looked at the mound of flowers one more time.

Nick refrained from reminding her she'd done that years ago when she'd slipped off into the night and married his father.

"Thank you, Nick. Thank you both," she included

Shelby in a heartfelt hand squeeze, "for coming with me."

"As long as you know," he said quietly, "we came for you. Not for him."

The cemetery had emptied except for Mr. Vaughn, who was standing with Leo, the chauffeur, and some of the staff from the funeral home. Nick guided Marsha and Shelby toward the car.

He didn't glance back as they left the cemetery. The man who had so obviously contributed to his gene pool had been such a fool. He'd thrown his daughter away; never bothered to get to know his father. As far as Nick was concerned, Shelby was wrong this time. He hadn't missed a thing in not knowing his grandfather.

Would his mother still be having kind thoughts when she realized the extremes he was willing to go to even now, to make them dance to his tune?

The joke's on you, old fool. He leaned back in the seat, looked at Shelby smugly and felt the triumphant surge of victory.

As soon as they arrived back at the house, Mr. Vaughn herded people toward the den for the reading of the Will. Then he told Marsha to take as much time as she needed. "Whenever you're ready," he told her and disappeared in the same direction everyone else had gone.

"Why do I get the feeling his 'whenever you're ready' means now?" Marsha commented with a dim smile.

"Take time if you need it, Mom." This was going to be difficult.

"Let's just get it over, shall we?"

Shelby, in her perfect little black dress, had turned as white as a sheet. Or maybe it was just the contrast with her red-rimmed eyes.

"If you're sure, lead the way," he suggested to his mom, taking Shelby's arm. Her hand shook when he entwined their fingers.

The marble-floored foyer ran the length of the house, with other halls and doors leading off it. Marsha finally opened the furthest.

Nick stopped Shelby outside as his mother went in. "What's the matter?"

She shook her head. "I can't quit shaking."

"Probably because you know what's coming," he said quietly then took a deep breath and squared his shoulders. Something inside him was shaking, too. "If it makes you feel any better, I'm not exactly looking forward to this, either." An ominous feeling settled over him with the words, but they must have helped Shelby. She propelled him into the room.

There were a couple dozen people gathered. Mostly past and present household employees, he decided, as Mr. Vaughn motioned the three of them to the long leather couch he'd saved at the front of the room. "We have a lot to get through," Vaughn said, clearing his throat, "so shall we get started?"

For the first time since they'd arrived, Nick thought of Christine. He looked around, wondering if she was in attendance. Had she even been at the funeral? He'd forgotten her.

A couple of the middle-aged women looked out of place. When he heard their bequests, Nick found his suspicions were well-founded. For their faithful "companionship," they both received an assortment of personal things from Chester Celinski and daggered looks from each other. His grandfather hadn't been a hermit or quite as "faithful" as he'd obviously expected his "companions" to be. Nick bit his lip to keep from smiling and Shelby gave him an identical, knowing look. His mother looked oblivious.

The list of generous financial bequests and personal items divided among the employees and a select number of friends seemed endless. From their pleased expressions mixed with sentimental tears, Nick gathered the old man had been a better employer and friend than father.

A two-story wall of windows overlooked a much more wild and wooded landscape than the neatly manicured and landscaped lawns out front. This was a room and a view he could get used to.

He knew in his gut this was where the old man had spent his time. Nick felt a surge of distaste for appreciating it as he realized this is also where the video had been filmed. The desk was the same. The bookcase behind had been a backdrop. What kind of man could make manipulative, vindictive plans—the list of his crimes was endless—in a room this pleasant?

The attorney cleared his throat and stood up behind the huge desk. "Those of you who have been mentioned already may leave. Mr. Celinski asked that the distribution of his assets to his family be private." His gaze seemed to rest pointedly on Shelby.

Nick tightened his hold on her hand. If anyone had an interest in what was coming, it was Shelby. And if Mr. Vaughn wanted to get technical, she hadn't been mentioned in the old man's Will. Wasn't that who he'd asked to leave?

The attorney met his eyes then looked down immediately to straighten his papers.

The woman who'd received the largest bequest stopped to push a button by the door and a soft whir sounded as the heavy drapes slowly closed. She also dimmed the lights.

Vaughn, who had seemed at ease until now, pranced from foot to foot. "This isn't as unusual as it was several years ago, but your father wanted to tell you about your inheritance himself," he directed to Marsha. "He put it on videotape. I hope this won't be too difficult for you."

She shook her head and looked at him trustingly.

The attorney turned to the built-in cabinets to one side. Opening a large door, he revealed a big screen television. "I wish people who feel they must 'reappear' one last time to their loved ones would realize how traumatic it can be."

"It's okay, Bradley." Her voice shook slightly. It was husky and ripe with tears waiting to be shed. "I assure you, I want to see my father one more time." She sank further into her end of the massive leather sofa they occupied and looked very small. "I think he would have known that."

"Come down here." Shelby, who was sitting between them, offered her hand and Marsha scooted to their end of the long couch without hesitation. Shelby scrunched closer under the arm Nick had extended behind her on the back of the couch, making it possible for him to reach his mother's shoulder. He cupped it reassuringly with one hand while Shelby held one of each of their hands. At last, they were a tightly knit threesome.

Mr. Vaughn took an audible breath and punched a button on the remote control.

The familiar still photos began. Nick had practically memorized them. Once Marsha recovered from her surprise, she started a sentimental monologue for Shelby, wallowing in the proud mother's opportunity to share Nick's childhood with his new wife. Shelby managed to make appropriate noises without giving away that she'd already seen them.

Nick heard his mother's sharp intake of breath the second Chester Celinski's image came onto the screen. The room went deathly still until the old man broke the silence.

"When was this taken?" Marsha asked quietly.

"A couple of weeks ago," the lawyer answered. "He updated everything then."

To an accompaniment of her muffled sobs, Chester proceeded to give his only daughter everything remaining in his estate. The house. Half interest in Celidon. His stocks, bonds and art collections. Marsha released one last anguished sob as he told her he loved her. Then he turned his attention to Nick.

"And to my favorite grandson, Nicholas Evans, Jr." Nick was his *only* grandson and the old man seemed to enjoy his little joke. Somewhere it registered that he'd called Nick by his father's name instead of trying to turn him into a "Chet."

Nick sat dazed, his mind flitting as he compared

this tape with the one at home. This version of the man was older by a couple of years, a lot more mellow and a little more frail.

"—don't have a thing you haven't gotten along without," his grandfather continued. "But since you'll probably get everything when Marsha's at this end of her life—may that be a long, long time away, my dear," he said in an aside, "I haven't left you much, Nick. My father's pocket watch and a little money. I won't go into details now since it's in trust funds I started a long time ago when you were born. Bradley will fill you in. Mostly it's a remembrance."

He chuckled as if the irony of the word amused him. "I hope my little gift helps you through some of the rough times we all face from time to time." He paused and sobered. "I haven't been much of a grandfather but I have loved you in my own way. From my long-distance observation of your life, your father and mother did a wonderful job of raising you and I'm very proud to be your grandfather.

"If there were two things I could wish for you, they would be the happiness your mother found with your father and the talent to avoid some of my mistakes."

Chester Celinski turned his attention back to his daughter. "I only have one regret, my dear Marsha—no, it isn't what you think. I did make mistakes but you can't regret those. My regret is that even though I realized I'd made those mistakes, I was too proud to admit it. By the time I was no longer proud, I was too close to this point in my life to offer apologies. They would have sounded exactly like what they were—pitiful blubberings from a dying old man.

I couldn't take the thought of having only your pity in the end.'' Marsha sobbed again. True to form, Shelby accompanied her. Nick swallowed hard to alleviate the painful block of tears in his own throat.

"I love you both," Chester Celinski said quietly. "I pray you both choose to be happy." He sketched the same salute to the camera with his feeble blue-veined hand. This time it was minus the wink. "Till we meet again in the next world..."

The screen flickered then turned gray.

Nick couldn't seem to unglue his gaze from it. His mother was crying in earnest, and he ought to comfort her. He couldn't even seem to clear his throat to say anything. He could hear the lawyer's heavy footsteps as he walked back to turn up the lights.

Nick's ability to move came back with the illumination.

Shelby sat twisting the ring on her finger as she also sat mesmerized by the blank screen, as stunned and in shock as he was. Her expression as she looked at him said it all. They were married for no reason.

The old coot hadn't uttered the words marriage or the name Christine throughout the entire tape! Marsha had inherited everything. No strings attached.

Shelby escaped an instant after she hugged Marsha and offered her congratulations. She didn't look at Nick again.

Nick stayed long enough to find out the details he needed to know about his inheritance and to convince his mom she should accept her good fortune. When he suggested the two of them probably had a lot of legal odds and ends to do, they had their heads together over paperwork before he got to the door.

"Oh." Mr. Vaughn remembered as Nick opened it. "Christine Donovan, your mother's business partner, will be here with her fiancé, Kevin Liedecker, for a late supper. Some of the papers transferring Celidon, you both have to sign," he explained to Marsha. "I know that makes it a long day for all of you, but I thought it would be better to get it over with all at once."

Marsha agreed and thanked him.

"I've asked the staff to serve dinner at eight-thirty," he told Nick, glancing at his watch. "We'll meet in the salon for drinks at eight?"

"Thank you." Nick idly thought he'd have to ask Michael which room was called the salon. "Shelby and I will be there." He would get to meet the woman whose name had struck terror into his heart until a half hour ago.

Nick let himself out of the den and leaned against the heavy solid wood door. He was married and didn't need to be. He let the reality sink in. For all intents and purposes, his association with Shelby was at an end. She was an unnecessary wife.

The conviction that they couldn't just end it now, though, zapped him at the same time. He wasn't sure why. He had to have time to think about it. It was all too complicated.

From the sound of things, his mother would have kissed the entire fortune off had the other tape been played. She was so afraid accepting it would be a betrayal of his father that a few minutes ago, she'd practically begged Nick to forgive her *if* she did take her inheritance.

"Dad would love this," Nick had told her. "He loved seeing right restored and the good guys win their just rewards. You know he'd be delighted for you, Mom." She'd thrown her arms around him and turned in her ticket on the guilt trip she'd been preparing to embark on.

And Christine had a fiancé. He'd bet his life she sent the tape. It seemed he had a lot to thank the woman for—an out-of-date tape, an unnecessary marriage.

It was a good thing he was "safely" married to Shelby, he thought with a wry twist to his lips.

"Safely" married. What a misnomer. What a mess. And for some reason, he felt on shakier ground now than he had through this whole experience.

He found Shelby as he started up the stairs. She was sitting halfway up the wide staircase at just the point it started to flare out on either side. She looked small and vulnerable against the dark background.

His heart flip-flopped at the sight of her. Guilt and regret, he explained the emotional tug. He'd put them through two days of hell for nothing. But it hadn't all been hell, something in him rebelled at the word. For the most part, she'd made it very pleasant.

She looked like a bewildered little girl. She'd changed clothes. She was shoeless. Her bare toes curled over the edge of the step her feet were on and he wondered how she could manage to make bare feet as sexy as anything he'd ever seen.

"Shelby?" He sank down beside her, one step below the stair she sat on. She meet his eyes and giggled.

His gaze hovered on a colorful butterfly decorating the knit top that hugged her curves lovingly. Shelby saw where his gaze was and sobered. A charge of awareness sizzled around and between them and he idly wondered what she'd do if he tried out a Rhett Butler routine. The image of hauling her into his arms and up the stairs to the bedroom was so graphic his mouth went dry. The fantasy certainly beat thinking about all this.

She shook her head in total amazement, as if she knew what he was thinking and started giggling again.

Not that Nick could see what was so funny. "I guess I don't have to worry that you're distraught with the news."

"You thought I'd be distraught at the idea of giving up this marriage?" There was something carefully derisive in her tone, something that offended him. "It's been an absolute calamity, start to finish. All two days of it."

He had the insane urge to argue with her.

"Boy, did we botch it," Shelby said.

They'd botched it. *He'd* botched it. He couldn't think of a thing to say.

"It's a good thing I saw the tape for myself," she said. "If I'd only seen this one without the benefit of the other, I would have thought…I don't know what I would have thought. It's not like you have such a fond regard for marriage that you'd trick me into it."

He ought to be laughing, too, agreeing with every word she said.

She shook her head. "The man today wasn't the same one on the tape at your house."

"I know." Nick tried to concentrate instead of feeling lost and dazed. "I think he must have made the other one several years ago."

"Did you manage to find out anything more?" She leaned an elbow on the step beside her and braced her cheek on her fist. The change in position angled her legs over his, not touching, just close enough to feel her warmth. Her face was suddenly nearer and her lips drew his attention.

"You mean about the change in the Will," he asked absently.

"No, I mean about your pocket watch," she said with the dry sarcasm he was coming to lo—like, he amended. "Of course I mean about the change in the Will," she finished.

"Mr. Vaughn admitted it changed in the last couple of weeks."

"That's all he said?"

"I couldn't exactly grill him about it," he said, matching his tone to hers. "Mom asked what her father updated and all Vaughn said was that Mom's inheritance hadn't changed, only the terms and conditions," he quoted.

"And we know what those terms and conditions were," Shelby supplied, holding out her hand to stare at the plain gold band on her finger. "So what's next? I guess this for starters," she murmured, taking it off.

He shrank away as if it was poisonous. Before he

had time to think about it again, he *did* the Rhett Butler thing. One arm went beneath the knees she'd made so convenient, the other behind her back. She was suddenly in his arms and he was carrying her up the stairs.

"Wha...?"

"We can't talk about it here," he muttered.

"But I can walk."

"I wouldn't want you to get a splinter." He looked pointedly at her bare feet.

"I've never seen such polished wood," she said. "It's as smooth as marble."

But he didn't put her down, even when they got to the carpeted hallway.

He stopped outside the closed door of their room and she waited for him to let her down then. "Just open the door," he suggested gruffly when she looked at him expectantly. She did as he asked and he carried her in and dumped her haphazardly on the bed.

"What was that about?" she asked breathlessly.

He wanted to follow her down and kiss her and himself senseless, forget this whole muddled mess. She asked far too many questions, questions he didn't have answers to. "It seemed like the thing to do at the time," he said. He backed away a step, put his hands on his hips to keep them off her.

Her eyes danced with amusement, her lips had parted in good humor. She crossed her legs, Indian-style, and tented one knee over the other.

"You can put that back on for starters," he suggested, nodding at the ring.

"But it's—"

"This marriage has to die a very natural death," he said.

"But wh—"

"We still don't know who sent the tape," he said, uncertain what that had to do with anything, but just as certain they couldn't end this as impulsively as they'd started. "We might get someone in trouble. And unless we want to complicate things for my mother, until every *i* is dotted and every *t* is crossed, we need to leave things as they stand."

"But—"

"We'll go back to Kansas City and let things fizzle gradually as far as everyone here is concerned."

This time, she didn't try to get a word in edgewise. She just scowled at him.

"Mom's made her peace with her dad." As he said it, he understood why they couldn't just come out with the truth. "What would it do to her if she saw the other tape?" That was what was troubling him, he thought thankfully, not the thought of...of...giving up Shelby.

"And she would insist on seeing it, wouldn't she," Shelby agreed, frowning.

"Even if we only told her, she'd be upset."

"She'd be devastated," Shelby supplied a more accurate word.

He paced. "So let's let the dust settle," he suggested quietly, stopping in front of her. "Then I'll drop hints that everything isn't right between us. In a couple of months I'll tell her you've moved out."

She suddenly looked so somber, he grinned. "I'll tell her my great expectations went to your head—"

she threw a pillow at him ''—and then grumble in-
cessantly while I'm giving you half my trust funds in
a divorce settlement.''

''So I get to be the bad guy?''

''Better you than me,'' he said facetiously. ''I do
have an inheritance of my own to look forward to if
I don't mess up like my mother did.'' He decided he
could trust himself to get closer. ''Seriously.'' He settled on the side of the bed. ''I want you to have half
the trust funds.''

''I don't want your trust funds,'' she muttered.

''How do you know? You don't know how much
it is.''

''I don't care.''

''You earned it. You should profit. Besides, you
don't know the details,'' he taunted again.

''Don't tell me.'' She held her hands to her ears
and cringed. ''I'm only human.''

How in the hell could she make him want her so
much, just being silly?

''I heard enough to know I don't *want* to know
what I'll be missing out on when my rich husband
dumps me.'' Her eyes were as wide as saucers and
she looked so adorable he wanted to...to...

He pulled her to the side of the bed and took her
into his arms. ''I'm only human,'' he half growled.
''And I *do* want to know what I'm missing.'' His
hand braced the back of her head as he kissed her.
For a second, she froze then her body went fluid in
his arms. His growl blended with her moan as the kiss
deepened.

Her hand flattened against his chest. He had on far

too many clothes. The suit was stifling, even though he'd long ago loosened the tie. He could feel his heart beat in the palm of her hand.

"This isn't good…"

"Then I'll have to do better," he murmured.

She did. Somehow, she turned the intensity to a honeyed sweetness that he knew he wouldn't forget. It was even more intense in its way. And his wanting turned to a soul-deep need.

Lacing his fingers through her soft hair, he lifted it from her neck and gave himself access to the silky skin there. He skimmed kisses behind her ear, halfway down her neck, in the hollow by her collarbone. He honed in on the butterfly covered breasts and started to ease her backward over his arm.

"No, Nick." She blew the protest by groaning it and sagging weakly back on the bed, holding on tight and taking him with her. She kissed him this time, but it became bittersweet. Her fingers lightly traced his face, his shoulders, then she clung to him. "Nick," she whispered on a trembling sigh.

But when his mouth recaptured hers again, he realized she'd grown limp in his arms. She was no longer participating.

With more will than he knew he had, he lifted himself slightly away and waited for her to open her eyes.

When she did, they were bright. Her kiss-swollen lips tilted at the corners. She lifted one finger and pushed a lock of his hair back in place. "I do want out of this eventually," she said huskily. "I'd rather it not be the classic case of marry in haste, repent at leisure. Let's be wise. Let's not have too much to repent," she pleaded.

He sagged to his side and propped his head on his fist.

"You turn me on like a light switch," she admitted, facing him from a distance. "But like you, I have my future to think of."

With one more glance in his direction, she scooted to the edge of the bed and picked up her sandals. "These aren't glass slippers," she muttered. "And I'm not Cinderella. I'm not going to kid myself that you're going to turn into the handsome prince and cart me off to your castle."

She was talking to herself again. He found it as charming and endearing as it was fascinating. He decided to let it slide that she didn't believe he was the handsome prince. He wouldn't point out that he'd "carted" her off to the best replica of a castle he knew.

She sighed and directed her next thought to him. "Since we're going to have to stay married for a while, maybe we could start thinking of practical, day-to-day things."

He frowned.

"—like food," she said. "I'm starving. You think we'd get in trouble if we raided the kitchen?"

He laughed, just as she'd intended. Then he dropped the bomb about the planned entertainment for the evening.

CHAPTER NINE

A TALL thin man was alone mixing himself a martini when Nick and Shelby entered the salon. "Can I get you a drink?" he offered, eyeing Shelby with the masculine appreciation Nick had noticed she earned everywhere she went. Nick placed a proprietary hand on her waist as the man explained that Christine, Marsha and Mr. Vaughn were still in the den signing papers.

"I said I'd tend bar until they get back," he continued. "Unless you want something complicated," he added. "Then we'll have to call Michael."

"White wine?" Shelby asked.

"I'll have a beer," Nick said.

"I think I can handle that," he said with a crooked grin.

"And you must be..."

"Kevin Liedecker." The temporary bartender dried his hand on a towel and stuck it across the bar. "Sorry. I knew who you were. I forgot you didn't have the same advantage. Christine's fiancé," he explained. "And this is the fabled grandson's new bride?"

"Shelby," Nick filled in, wondering about the slightly cynical "fabled."

"Newlyweds, I hear?" Kevin handed Shelby her wine.

"Yes." Shelby answered the question without saying how long they'd been married. She rewarded the curiosity in his voice with some of her own. "When do you and your fiancée plan to be married?"

Kevin shrugged thoughtfully and poured Nick's beer. "Haven't really had a chance to set a date. We just got around to getting engaged."

"Oh?" Nick and Shelby asked at the same time.

Kevin replied pointedly, "Yesterday," and Nick's suspicion that Christine had sent him the original tape seemed to be confirmed. Wasn't it too much of a coincidence that he and Christine got engaged the day he and Shelby got married.

"We made it official when Brad informed us Christine didn't have to attend the reading of Chet's Will this afternoon." He demolished Nick's reasoning about the timing while verifying the motivation. They wouldn't have known his marriage had let her off the hook. But they would have known it was significant that she was no longer mentioned in the Will.

"Are you testing us in some way? Trying to see what we know?" Shelby asked.

Nick used wiping his first sip of beer off his lip as an excuse to hide his smile. Shelby's refusal to beat around the bush for too long with anyone was one of the things he admired about her.

Kevin laughed, obviously appreciating the characteristic, too. He held his glass up to Shelby. "Smart lady," he toasted her.

"Christine sent the tape?" Shelby asked in a whisper.

"What tape?" Kevin's innocent tone contradicted his expression.

Nick eased down onto one of the bar stools as Shelby leaned closer to him. He braced her against his side. "A videotape of my grandfather," he answered Kevin's question.

Kevin offered a practiced frown. "A videotape?"

"Legal stuff," Nick stated abruptly.

"How would Christine have access to your grandfather's legal things? Unless you thought it was me—" Before either of them could formulate an answer, he raised a finger as if he'd just remembered something. "Oh. I'll bet you heard I used to be a law clerk at Carmichael, Cole and Vaughn," he added significantly.

"As in Bradley Vaughn?" Nick managed to find his tongue.

"You're every bit as bright as your wife, I see." Kevin idly thumped at the olive floating in his glass then looked at both of them with renewed innocence. "I guess you haven't heard I quit that job almost a year ago."

"How would we know—" Shelby started.

"There are some things you just can't feel good about," he continued as if Shelby hadn't said a thing.

"Like sending—"

"There are also some things better left unsaid," he added, interrupting Nick. When both of them were speechless, he raised his glass to them. For the first time he sobered. "I hope I can toast the *happy* new couple?"

"I hope you'll wait for us," Nick's mother said

from the doorway. "I haven't had the chance to do that yet, myself."

Marsha looked more than a little weary, but behind the tired exterior, her eyes were glowing. Every bit of the past two days had been worth the hassle, Nick thought, looking from his mother to Shelby. She didn't have the emotional commitment he did, but he hoped she felt a bit of the satisfaction.

Shelby's soft smile reassured him and made him want to kiss those fascinating upturned lips in gratitude. Then she turned it on Kevin as if to show him *she,* for one, was onto his game and had no hard feelings. And that's what he'd been fishing for, Nick felt certain. Kevin had made a monumental miscalculation in sending the tape and if they'd gotten married because of it, he was anxious to make amends. Or at least find out where he stood.

He'd taken a big chance. The risk he'd taken in all but confessing just now was even bigger. If Nick and Shelby chose to, they could make his life miserable. But Nick couldn't find it in his heart to hold any of it against him. He'd only tried to keep a wrong from being committed. Even though their marriage had been unnecessary, the original goal had been achieved. His mother and Christine had inherited what they should. And Shelby had turned out to be a totally unexpected and valuable bonus.

"Make us a drink, Kev," a new voice said. "We'll *all* toast the happy couple…and all sorts of promising partnerships."

Nick would have willingly testified in court that nothing could further shock him today. He would have been committing perjury, he realized as Mr. Vaughn and a woman entered behind his mother.

"C.J.?" he managed to exclaim.

The very familiar woman beside Mr. Vaughn let her grin spread from her lips to her eyes. "Hi, Nick," she said affectionately. "It's been awhile, hasn't it?"

Christine was as beautiful as she'd been fifteen years ago. She was petite, a good six inches shorter than Shelby. She had dark, dark eyes and long dark hair that looked as shiny and rich as an oriental carpet. He didn't think she'd aged a day. But she'd gone by C.J. then, not Christine. And not once had it entered his mind that C.J. Donovan might be *the* Christine his grandfather had mentioned on the tape. Christine Donovan. In a million years he would have never associated the two. He racked his mind to remember what she'd told him about herself when they dated in college.

Her father had died in Vietnam after some woman—his mother? he wondered with a start—had dumped him. Her mother had been Vietnamese and had let the rich American soldier's family adopt her baby since mixed children had little hope of having a decent life in their native land.

C.J.'s life couldn't have been easy, he thought with the same rush of sympathy he'd had when she'd told him the story, though she'd probably never wanted for anything. She sauntered over to give him a warm hug.

"Your mother says you build houses now," she said conversationally as Kevin began making drinks for the newcomers.

"Beautiful houses," Shelby said beside him.

"You must be Shelby." C.J. graciously extended her hand.

Nick made the introductions. Shelby's gaze locked with his in total bewilderment. "You two know each other...from?"

"College. We bummed around a lot together," Christine answered Shelby's question, making it sound a lot less friendly than it had been. C.J. was the one woman he'd convinced himself he had been in love with—until Shelby!

The thought sideswiped him.

He loved Shelby? They hadn't been... He hadn't known her... Two days! You couldn't love someone after two days.

Unless it was Shelby, a voice argued in his head.

The two of them together carried on a tentative, feel-each-other-out conversation, and he realized he couldn't fight the word or the thoughts off any longer. He did love Shelby. What he'd felt for C.J. had been lukewarm compared to the white-hot, dizzy euphoria he felt with Shelby. That first sweet kiss...even thinking about it made his mouth water and his body react. The contentment he felt holding her...just being with her... The word wasn't adequate. Happiness didn't describe it, either. Not even close.

The feeling had sneaked up on him and nothing in his past experience had prepared him for the intensity. He felt it as physically as he'd ever felt any tackle in a football game. And the discovery left his mind as scrambled as the most devastating blow.

Shelby turned to respond to something Marsha said

and C.J. moved closer. "Your wife is very pretty," she complimented as Shelby gravitated down the bar toward his mother. He felt a compelling need to follow.

"Thank you." Watching her left him short of breath. In the time they'd had to get ready, Shelby had pulled her usually well-mannered hair to the top of her head and let it fall in a loose cascade of curls. The style bared even more skin and displayed the long line of her elegant neck. She looked even more regal than the night she'd helped him choose panty hose. He couldn't begin to think which version of Shelby Wright he preferred: the arrogant knock-'em-dead blue-jeans-clad wise guy or the dignified beauty. Pride mingled with the bright, unexpected, unnameable emotion surging in his heart.

He forced himself to look at C.J. "*You* are still very beautiful." The sentiment was sincere even if she couldn't hold a candle to Shelby.

"And you haven't changed a bit." C.J.'s smile held amusement. She tried to raise herself to one of the tall stools gracing the bar. She was short and her calf-length red dress was fitted. Nick helped her up then lounged back against the seat he'd vacated.

"You aren't having regrets that you didn't wait and marry me then?" Christine asked as Kevin handed Mr. Vaughn a drink and drew him into a conversation of their own.

Nick's gaze held onto the scene at the end of the bar where Shelby was talking with his mother. "I love my wife," he said simply.

"I could tell," Christine admitted, sipping her wine.

"Could you?"

"The sparks coming from your eyes when you look at her are a good hint," she said with a chuckle. "I imagine they'd turn to arrows if she was talking to a man the intimate way she's talking to your mother."

"I'll have to be less obvious."

He didn't miss Christine's raised eyebrow. "Who do you want to hide it from? Her?"

The elation spinning through him turned to massive confusion. He didn't have a clue what Shelby felt. That realization filled him with a stunned dismay. "Why would I want to do that?" he finally managed to say.

"What's the matter?" Christine's voice held her concern.

"Nothing." He shook his head. "Nothing. I think I'm in shock."

She laughed quietly. "It's been that kind of day, huh?"

He nodded and changed the subject to one that would let him think coherently. "Did you know who I was in college?"

"Sure. Why do you think I came to KU?"

"Why'd you quit after one semester? Why didn't you stay? You just disappeared."

"I could see the writing on the wall." She traced the engraved pattern on her wineglass. "You'd already told me you weren't going to quit school and come to work for my grandfather," she said.

A piece of their shared history clicked into place.

If he'd done what she'd asked, he would have been
working for his grandfather, too.

"Besides, I was needed here," Christine added.
"That's when Grandfather's health began to decline.
You tell me," she went on, "what was a college ed-
ucation going to do for me?"

She had a point, he realized. He'd bet she was one
of the youngest female CEOs in the country. She
probably learned more putting in her time with their
grandfathers than she could ever have learned at a
university. If he'd learned one thing from his teaching
stint, it was that the best way of learning was by doing.

"Why'd you come in the first place?" They were
speaking in low tones, leaning toward each other. He
was glad no one seemed to mind. Christine felt like
unfinished business, a part of his life he had to put an
ending on before he could go on. He glanced at
Shelby.

"I'd been waiting to marry you since I was a
child," Christine said, regaining his attention. "Some
of my earliest memories are of our grandfathers talking about our marriage and the dynasty we would create. Your grandfather showed me pictures of you regularly. I would have known you anywhere." She
reached to trace his jawline with the back of her bright
red fingernail. "I decided it was time to find out if I
was satisfied with my 'destiny.'"

His mouth twitched.

"I liked it," she admitted. "I was in love with the
idea of loving you before we ever met. I was impatient and I wanted to force the issue. But I had just

enough idealism left in me at the time to want you to *choose* me instead of being forced to take me.''

"I *did* choose you,'' he said, wanting to stroke the ego that must have been as bruised as his had been. "You didn't want me if I remember correctly.''

"You wanted to teach.'' Her tone dismissed the profession as disdainfully as she'd dismissed it then. "I thought you might as well get it out of your system before we got married rather than while.'' She laughed. "It isn't like I didn't know I'd get you eventually. And my ego was fragile. I figured if you wouldn't do what I wanted, you couldn't care about me as much as I wanted you to. I was in my manipulative phase at the time,'' she finished with a derisive shrug. "Our grandfathers taught me well.''

"They were two frustrated old men who must have been terribly unhappy to want so badly to control everyone else's lives.''

"I loved my grandfather dearly.'' Her wistful tone revealed that she missed him even now. "Even if he was a domineering old coot.''

She used the word lightly but meant it seriously, Nick suspected.

"Neither of them could help it, you know? You'd have to understand how hard they worked to create all this...how bewildering the world was becoming for them. They came from societies where the patriarch of the family knew everything, even if he knew nothing.''

"You're more generous than I am,'' Nick said.

"Let's just say I learned. Just as I learned how and when to manipulate them right back. It was easy to cope with their demands that way. In the end, I had them both wrapped around my finger."

He didn't doubt it for an instant. And though he'd attributed his desire to avoid the state of matrimony to her, he knew Christine had done him a favor. At the tender age of twenty, he'd been all too anxious to mold himself into the picture of domesticity his father had been. But he hadn't been ready. Or truly in love with her. He suspected her "in love with the idea of being in love" analysis applied to him as well.

The quiet emotionless argument they'd had right before she'd left for Christmas had never been resolved. He'd thought it would be when she returned to campus after semester break. When she hadn't, didn't even contact him, his taste for marriage had been bitter.

Looking back, his biggest revelation should have come when he had quickly moved on. Within weeks he'd been interested in someone else—confirmation that he wasn't cut out for marriage or the unselfishness it might require.

"Did you get my grandfather to change his Will?" Nick lowered his voice even more, realizing it wouldn't be impossible for someone to overhear their quiet conversation.

"I didn't know he did it," she said, moving the drink she'd barely touched to one side. "I was still prepared to marry you."

"But you're marrying Kevin instead? Isn't your change of heart a bit sudden?"

She looked affectionately at the man across the bar. "I love Kevin," she said. "He did what he did for me," she added with a subtle plea in her voice. "I hope you and Shelby were already planning this wedding."

He didn't want to get into that with Christine, either. It didn't matter anyway. What's done was done. "You love Kevin, but you were going to marry me?"

"We could have shared a name, maybe an address if you wanted. I would have gone my way, allowed you to go yours." She laughed at the surprised look on his face. "That's what I meant about learning to cope with our grandfathers' demands. There's always some way to get around things."

"And Kevin was satisfied with that?"

"Kevin loves me—but he loves my fortune, too," she added as if it was matter-of-fact. "He wouldn't have asked me to give that up. Why do you think he smuggled that copy of the tape from old man Vaughn's office? He's good at figuring how to get what he wants without giving up a thing."

"But he didn't know it had changed?"

"He had no way of knowing. That must have been recent. Neither of us knew a second tape existed," she admitted. "He copied the one he sent you shortly after it was made. He smuggled it home last year when Chet started being sick all the time. And he quit his job at the law firm shortly after that." She smiled affectionately toward him. "Said he could no longer be trusted. Until yesterday when Bradley told us, we thought it was still Chet's last will and testament."

"You could have warned me sooner," he said dryly.

Christine's expression turned to one of contentment. "Kevin didn't know how badly he wanted me until it came right down to the wire," she said. "When push came to shove, he didn't want to share me. Not even with you." She sighed blissfully. "I needed this."

Nick was glad she wouldn't wonder the rest of her life whether her major attraction was herself or her fortune. She'd know Kevin loved her.

"He didn't tell me he was sending the tape until after it was done because I might have stopped him."

"Why?"

"I can't bear the thought of him getting in trou-. ble," she said simply. "Marriage is just a piece of paper." She reached and patted Nick's hand. "I thought I could have stood to be married on paper to you while I shared my heart and soul with him. But ask me *now* if I'm still ready to marry you?"

"Are you ready to marry me now, C.J.?"

"Not a chance. I want everything *plus* the legal piece of paper."

He glanced down the bar to find Shelby watching him and Christine with suspiciously bright eyes.

"You suppose we should quit acting like this is our own private reunion," Christine said with a smile in the same direction.

"That might be a good idea," Nick agreed as Mr. Vaughn put on his officiating tone and made the first toast. "To Celidon and a successful new partnership between these two lovely ladies."

By the time everyone but Shelby had offered toasts, she looked slightly giddy. But she insisted she had one, too. ''To dinner,'' she offered succinctly.

''To dinner,'' everyone wholeheartedly agreed.

Dinner went well. His mother and C.J.—or Christine. He was having trouble deciding which to call her— spent the time finding common ground and discussing, in general terms, how they would work together. Mr. Vaughn and Kevin threw out advice from time to time, both legal and otherwise.

Then attention focused on Shelby as she told them about her business.

''You never did say why you quit teaching,'' Christine said when the first lull came in the conversation. ''As determined as you were to go into it, I couldn't believe it when Marsha told me you weren't doing it anymore.''

''It got too complicated,'' he answered vaguely.

''What Nick went through makes it totally understandable why there are no male teachers at the elementary level,'' his mother said loquaciously.

Nick groaned inwardly.

''What happened?'' Kevin asked.

''One of the little girls in his class had a crush on him—well, most of them actually,'' his mother explained somewhat smugly.

''Not too surprising,'' Christine said.

Shelby didn't say a word.

''One of them fantasized to her friends that Nicholas had kissed her. But it was all straightened out and the poor child admitted that she'd made it up to impress her friends.''

''But in the meantime,'' his mother said, ''Nick was suspended.''

"So you quit," Christine stated.

Nick lifted a shoulder and still felt the guilt he'd felt at the time when he'd remembered Christine. He'd refused to give it up for her but when it came down to it, he'd given it up easily. "I considered moving to a lower grade, but my heart had gone out of it, I have to admit."

"He loves building houses," Shelby said. "He'd never quit doing that in the summer, even when he was teaching."

He tried to give her a grateful smile but she didn't meet his eyes.

"You wouldn't like to build them here in St. Louis?" his mother asked hopefully, picking up on a comment Mr. Vaughn had made earlier about wishing Shelby's business was in St. Louis.

"I think we've had more than enough changes in the past few days," Nick answered. "Maybe we should just sit back and let things settle before anyone makes any more big decisions."

When they rose to adjourn back to the salon, Shelby hovered by the door. "Speaking of settling…it has been a very long day. You wouldn't believe what time Nick got me up this morning."

The room stilled and she blushed furiously as she realized that everyone had jumped to the obvious conclusions. "You wouldn't mind if I called it quits for the evening, would you, Marsha?" she said in a rush.

"Of course not, my dear." She hurried back to where Shelby was standing and they exchanged a warm hug.

Nick could hardly wait to get her alone in their

room. He couldn't wait to... He swallowed hard, knowing he hadn't had a chance to think anything through. Should he just tell her? Take his chances? Seduce her?

She put a hand on his arm. "You and your mother haven't had any time at all together. You have old acquaintances to renew." Her eyes cut to Christine. "Stay." Her eyes pleaded. "Please?"

Torn between wanting to be alone with her and needing time to think things through, he let her issue her happy-to-meet-yous and good-nights, then walked her to the stairs.

"Shelby?"

"Yes," she asked when he didn't continue.

He had no idea how to continue. And how could he be so certain...it had been a day and a half. Could you fall in love with someone in thirty-six hours? Could you know the feeling was true when you'd only dealt with them in once-in-a-lifetime circumstances?

He gave up trying to think of words and touched her instead.

What did he have to offer someone like Shelby, who'd made it clear that stability—a family, a home—was exactly what she wanted. He moved frequently. Changed vocations when the mood struck.

She took a deep breath and stepped away from him. "I guess I'll say good night."

"I'll be up—"

"Don't hurry," she said, pressing her fingers against his mouth. "This will be easier," she reminded him of the sleeping arrangements.

"That's why you're going to bed now?"

"Partly." The full-fledged grin sneaked onto her pale face. "But I am very tired. Have you forgotten how hectic and sleepless the past couple of days have been?"

Mr. Vaughn came out of the salon, clearing his throat loudly and offering a mumbled "Sorry," as he put his head down and turned toward the den.

"You know what he thinks we're doing, don't you?" He didn't wait for her answer. "It would be a shame to disappoint him."

Her mouth raised automatically but she would have turned away at the last second if Nick hadn't trapped her lips with his.

He felt triumphant when they parted and she melted against him, releasing a resigned sigh. The sound reflected his feelings exactly. Total helplessness.

Her kiss drugged and dazed him, heightening every physical sensation while the rest of the world went away. His hands felt rough against her satiny skin so he buried them in the mass of tumbling curls. And though kissing her whetted his appetite for other things, he thought he'd be content kissing her from now until eternity.

He was spellbound, dazzled, bewildered and head over heels in love with her. Two days, two weeks or two hundred years wouldn't make a difference. He moved his hands down her shoulders and tried to mold her closer. She was as close as she could get. She felt like liquid gold in his arms.

Her breath came in a gasp as she tore her lips away. "I...I...think that's enough show for anyone," she said hurriedly, refusing to meet his gaze.

''I think I've fallen in love with you,'' he murmured.

Her startled eyes finally locked with his. They were wide and green and bright. She blinked and whatever he'd seen for a second there was cloaked behind a dull glaze.

''Don't get delusional on me now, Nick,'' she said thickly. With another quick good-night, she turned and ran up the stairs.

CHAPTER TEN

DELUSIONAL? Shelby thought he was delusional? The statement was still bugging Nick when he crawled into bed beside her a couple of hours later.

He told her he was in love with her and her only reaction was *that?*

She was sound asleep, her back to his side of the bed. He propped himself up and watched her several minutes, hoping she might be faking.

If she was faking, she certainly wouldn't let her mouth hang open that way. Her tiny little snores were cute, but he didn't imagine they could be fake. It irritated the heck out of him that he still thought she was beautiful when she thought he was crazy.

She *was* sound asleep. And he didn't *want* to stay on his side of the huge bed as they'd agreed. Since he was "delusional" anyway, he might as well delude himself into thinking she wanted him to hold her as much as he wanted to, he thought as he turned out the light.

Soft moonlight filtered through the sheer drapes and let him see her smile softly as he hovered over her. He studied her, left a kiss on her cheek, then carefully formed himself to her body. He had the exquisite sensation that life was suddenly as perfect as only she could make it seem. Okay, so he was delusional. But he no longer cared. She felt right in his arms. No single act had ever been so satisfying.

She was out of the room by the time he woke the next morning. By the time their flight left at two that afternoon, he'd received her message loud and clear: Shelby didn't plan to spend a minute alone with him.

She probably didn't want to deal with him if he got "delusional" again.

She couldn't avoid him on the plane, he thought impatiently, as their flight was called and they both kissed his mother goodbye.

His frustration level only increased when, as soon as they'd settled, Shelby took off his ring and held it out to him. His grip tightened on the arm of his seat.

"That's yours," he said. "What would I do with it?"

"Hold it for safekeeping? Keep it as a souvenir? Give it to someone else? I don't know."

He took it, turned her hand over and pressed it into her palm. "It's your souvenir," he said succinctly, folding her fingers around the wedding band. She shrugged, opened her purse and irreverently plopped it inside.

He clenched his teeth. "If nothing else, you can use it as a prop sometime. You never know when it might come in handy in your business to pretend you're married. Maybe you can start a whole new area of service."

"But I won't have to pretend, will I," she said sweetly, then studiously listened to the attendant talk about using the seat cushion as a flotation device.

"Have the last two days been that bad?" he finally asked.

"It hasn't been good or bad," Shelby murmured. "But it's over. Thank God," she added, flagging down the flight attendant to tell her she didn't feel comfortable sitting in the emergency aisle. She wasn't sure she could handle the situation if there was an accident. The attendant immediately went to make arrangements to change her seat.

"You're the most capable person I've ever known," he protested. "Why are you doing this, Shelby? What have I done to upset you?"

She intently gathered her things. "Nothing. I'm not upset."

"You didn't asked to be changed coming," he said pointedly.

"We weren't sitting in the emergency aisle," she said as the attendant returned with a "capable" volunteer to exchange places with her.

Nick had the pleasure of sitting next to a gregarious computer nerd who wanted to educate him on the joys of some new computer language.

By the time they touched down after the short haul to Kansas City, Nick was as determined that he didn't love her as he was convinced that he did. Somehow, while taking her home, his heart decided, *she* would show him she cared about him and this all would be fixed.

Shelby had been moved several rows behind him so he was out of the plane first. As soon as he was clear of the jetway, he stepped aside, out of the flow of traffic into the terminal.

She came toward him as soon as she crossed the threshold into the building, her smile firmly fixed. "Thanks for getting this for me," she said brightly. She took her garment bag out of his hand before he could reply. "Thanks, Nick. Thanks for everything."

"Shelby," someone called and Nick turned to see an attractive blond stud waving at her from twenty feet away.

"My ride's here," she said, refusing to meet his eyes. "Gotta go. I'll send you a bill. Call me if you need anything," she added breathlessly and brushed a kiss in the general direction of his cheek. Before he could recover from his dazed stupor, she hurried away.

Dammit, she was not going to do this, he thought, striding after her. Every single person in the airport conspired to keep him from catching her. He dodged and darted bodies but by the time he got to the place she and her "friend" had been, they were thirty yards away and on their way through the doors to the outside.

Nick slashed his hand through his hair and didn't mind that he'd left it standing on end. His hand slid down to rest on his neck and he rubbed at the knots there. He *didn't* love her. She was right. He'd been delusional. It had been a figment of his imagination. He wasn't even sure he liked her right now.

Shelby was a figment of his imagination. He'd dreamed her and it was time to wake up from the nightmare.

What was it with women? When he didn't feel the least bit interested, they clung like Krazy Glue. The two times he *thought* it wasn't a figment of his imagination and that he was falling in love, they did magical vanishing acts.

Dammit. Shelby wasn't going to get by with it.

Nick wanted to hit something; he wanted to yell at somebody; he wanted to wring the blond guy's neck.

By the time he got to the long-term parking lot where they'd left his car, he was seething. He tossed his money at the man in the toll booth and tore out of the lot, not waiting for his change.

Shoot. He had money now. His dear grandfather had made sure he'd never have any real money worries again. He didn't need the sixty cents the attendant owed him. And he didn't need a woman to tell him how to spend it.

He didn't need a woman, period.

Except Shelby. The words pierced his heart.

He didn't notice the red flashing lights in his rearview mirror until the police officer hit his siren a couple of times to get his attention. Nick smiled until his cheeks hurt and said, ''Yes, Officer'' so many times he almost drowned out the string of expletives playing in his mind. Now he was driving like Shelby. That was obviously going to get him nothing but trouble.

By the time the cop had written out his ticket, given him his lecture and let him go, Nick was at least seeing clearly again.

He'd hired her to do a job, for God's sake! She'd done it, and done it well. He'd gotten more than he'd expected. Couldn't he be grateful for that?

If he still thought he…might be interested in her in a couple of weeks or months, well, maybe he'd check her out again. He'd let things ride. Let the business arrangement die. Wait for the annulment. When the decks were cleared, maybe he'd take her out a few times…see what happened. But by that time, he probably wouldn't care.

He had to turn up the radio to drown out the voice in his head arguing that he really *was* being delusional now.

He slowed to turn into his driveway. Punching the garage door opener above his visor, he saw the key-less entry key pad and thought of Shelby.

Once inside the barren, impersonal house, he thought of Shelby.

He'd moved into this big empty house because it had been on the market six months without selling. He'd liked the unusual floor plan, and had intended using it again until this house didn't go quickly. Now it was time to move into something more single-man size. He'd cut the price. Or have a decorator in, as two Realtors had recommended.

Maybe he'd hire—

No! He wasn't going to think of her and her 'nesting' instincts and her desire to decorate his house.

The vise that seemed to have hold of his heart tightened.

He tossed his bag on the floor. Damn. Standing in the middle of the kitchen with his hands on his hips, he determinedly put her out of his mind.

But she didn't leave.

He was making a fool of himself over a woman he would tire of quickly in normal circumstances.

The indignant voice in his head got louder.

Anything he'd felt for her would fade as quickly as his imagined feelings for C.J. had. Outta sight, outta mind.

He bent and unzipped his bag. He didn't have any household staff around now to unpack and put things away. Good thing. He needed to keep busy for the next couple of days. Unpacking, taking the messages off his answering machine and a couple of loads of laundry were exactly the kinds of busywork he needed to get his mind firmly fixed back in the real world.

The Princess's kingdom had been restored. All was right with the world. Just because he'd been part of his mother's drama didn't mean he lived in a fairy tale now. *This* was the real world. And his real world didn't include Shelby!

His hand closed over something hard—not the soft pack of dirty laundry he expected—in his bag. The videotape he pulled out took him by surprise. He wasn't sure why, he thought wryly. He should be getting used to these kinds of surprises by now.

He hefted it. Should he watch it and get the bad news over with or should he set it on the counter for a couple of days and let the suspense build.

There was a large sticky note attached to one side. From his mom:

Dearest Nick,
Hope you don't mind me having Michael stick this in your bag for me. Bradley thought you might want a copy since it's the only way you'll ever know your grandfather.
  I was afraid you'd say you weren't interested if

I handed it to you. Someday you might be. Promise you'll keep it? Love to you and Shelby. She's a sweetheart, by the way. No wonder you love her. I do, too.

Mom

He tossed the tape in with the other one. Shoot, he'd start a collection. If his kids ever wanted to "meet" their great-grandfather...

He groaned and closed his eyes. He could still smell her subtle, clean, breath-of-fresh-air fragrance in the air.

That was delusional, his imagination. But he could pretend, couldn't he?

The vise had changed to a rock. Where his heart had been, there was now something heavy and painful. And now he was thinking of kids. Not just any kids. His and Shelby's.

He wanted them all to have her quick smile. Maybe a couple of them could have her tawny beige hair. The thought of the panty hose made him grin, but it came with an ache.

Maybe another kid or two could have his dark hair—without the cowlick. That was one gene his grandfather could have kept. "If you were going to regret something, you silly old man, you should have regretted that," he muttered to thin air.

His grandfather had had plenty to regret. For the first time since this had started, Nick felt sorry for the crazy old man. What must it have been like, wandering that monstrous house by himself for years? Being too stubborn for too long? Not doing something to fix things because he didn't want pity?

Nick thought of the two mistresses. Obviously his grandfather had not cared deeply for either of them. He'd let real love slip away because of pride. Was that Nick's real legacy from the old man?

C.J. had helped. His pride had let him convince himself he wasn't cut out for marriage. And he'd cultivated his selfishness as an excuse.

His grandfather had wished Nick the "happiness your mother found with your father and the talent to avoid some of my mistakes."

He wouldn't have the happiness without Shelby, no matter how much he tried to deny it. Did he love her? Yes. Did he want her to share his life? Three days of being with her and he was no longer sure he could survive without her. At least he had to know how she felt.

Maybe she was as terrified of her feelings for him as he was of his for her. Or probably, he forced himself to think realistically, she didn't want to be in the position of trying to let him down easy. She had a gentle spirit. She cared for everyone. Even his grandfather—the man who'd prompted her marriage to him through sneaky tricks—had earned some of her tears.

The only thing stopping him from telling Shelby how he felt was his inherited pride…and not knowing where she lived.

Her business card only included her phone number—exactly as he'd remembered. He called the number twice and got her answering machine. Deep in his gut, Nick knew she was home. He could *feel* her at the other end of that ringing phone.

She wasn't listed in the phone book. She said she lived a block and a half from the store. There were only so many directions you could go to get "a block and a half from the store." She lived in a duplex. Oscar the Dog barked when she had company. Her neighbor in the other half of the duplex was…was… It didn't matter. He didn't need to know her neighbor's name or to remember every detail Shelby'd told him to find her.

She'd given him the one clue he needed and he'd recognize her car. If there were eight more just like it in a two-block radius of the store, well, all he had to do was get out of his car and look inside each. When he found the one that looked lived-in, he'd know he'd found Shelby.

The worst she could do after he'd made a case for himself was turn him down.

He picked his car keys off the hook inside the back door.

The worst Shelby could do was turn him down. The thought froze his heart.

Her duplex was on the second street he tried. The builder had made it easy to tell which unit was which since the driveways were separated by the dual house. Oscar the Dog went nuts in the other side of the duplex as Nick parked and started up Shelby's walk. "Friend, Oscar," he muttered. "I wouldn't hurt her."

Her porch light came on and Shelby peeked out,

almost as soon as he knocked. She looked stunned and opened the door hesitantly.

"Nick?" Her hand clasped her throat. "What are you doing here?"

"I thought I'd check and make sure my 'wife' made it home safe and sound since you wouldn't let me bring you." He crossed his arms over his chest. "Aren't you going to invite me in?"

"How...how did...you find me?" She'd obviously thought about him not having her address.

He couldn't help but smile. He wasn't sure *what* that fact told him, only that it was significant. He pushed past her not waiting any longer for an invitation. "I drove a block and a half every direction from the grocery store until I found your car."

"Oh." She chewed at the corner of her lip. "What...?"

"Do I want?"

She nodded.

Finally ready to confront her, he suddenly lost some of his nerve. He'd seen signs that she felt at least some of the way he did, but she was one terrific actress. And he *was* delusional. He was no longer sure if he could tell what was real and what was fantasy. "Why didn't you *want* me to know where to find you?" he asked.

She turned, signaling him to follow her into her small living room.

The house felt like Shelby. Inviting. Airy. Comfortable. Her scent lingered in the air. A light green striped wallpaper, accented with an occasional darker stripe, gave the living room the ambience of an outdoor garden. Floral touches and plants enhanced the feel. It was cool, pleasant.

"You could have called." She didn't answer the question.

"I did."

She glanced up at him as her face took on a rosy pink flush. "I didn't get your message."

"I didn't leave one. I thought it would be better to say what I wanted to say in person." He took a step toward her and she evaded him, slipping behind the glass-and-wrought-iron coffee table.

Sitting down at one end of the couch, she indicated the other end for him. "You wanna sit down?"

He sank to the edge and she popped up like a jack-in-the-box.

"Can I get you something to drink? What would you like?" Her hands flailed aimlessly until she folded her arms self-consciously across her waist.

"Nothing, thanks."

Instead of sitting back down, she wandered to the window on the other side of the room where she idly picked a brown leaf off one of her hanging plants. "What was it you said you wanted?"

He couldn't talk to her back. He couldn't talk from so far away. He wasn't sure he could continue to stay in the same room with her without touching her. In two giant steps, he was within touching distance but she backed away.

"Shelby, why are you running from me?"

She started to deny it. He reached across the foot separating them and shushed her with one finger. "Why did you call your 'friend' to pick you up at the airport?'' he asked. Now that he was finally touching her he couldn't quit. He stroked her face, letting his fingers linger. ''Is he someone special to you?''

She looked at him, started to open her mouth again then the corners of her mouth drooped. She wanted to lie to him and she couldn't, he thought with a degree of tenderness he didn't think was possible.

''Shelby,'' he said softly. ''Oh, Shelby. Do you know I've been waiting my lifetime for you? I didn't think I ever wanted to be in love. I knew I didn't want to depend on someone for my happiness. But do you know how much I need you to make my life complete?''

Her eyes clouded and her expression folded in such a look of distress that he was suddenly terrified. For a second he thought his declaration might make her cry. He should have left it alone. She *didn't* care. She didn't know how to tell him.

''Oh, Nick, we can't both go off the deep end,'' she murmured. ''One of us has to be practical. We…you and I got an overload these past few days. Not much sleep. Too much emotion. The tape. The funeral. You seeing Christine. A wedding ring and…saying the words.'' She stumbled over that one. ''Sharing a room.'' Her voice fell to a whisper. ''You're imagining…we're imagining this,'' she amended. ''It was all too much. It made it seem real. We'll get—''

''Don't say it,'' he protested, pulling her close and cradling her in his arms. ''Don't you say I'll get over you. I won't.''

"But you don't love me," she protested. "And you wan—"

He couldn't resist her any longer. "How do you know?" he asked softly, studying her bright eyes. "Tell me, what do I feel if this need to be with you isn't love. You were in my house five minutes and it feels empty now without you."

His lips grazed hers tenderly. He sensed her in-drawn breath more than heard it. "I can't look at any-thing without thinking of you." A heady dizziness made him feel as if he would float away if she pressed closer. Her mouth clung to his, deepening the kiss. Magical, mystical heat roared through his veins and stabbed his heart until the beat quickened. "I've been thinking kindly of my grandfather because he brought us together," he added wryly. He finally forced him-self to push her slightly away. "If that isn't love, what is it?"

"Lust?"

"I might have thought that two days ago," he ad-mitted, kissing her again, nibbling. "Last night, when I held you in my arms all night—as much as I would have liked to make love to you—the important thing was having you there. You made all that other stuff, all the things you just listed seem manageable."

"You needed me because of a crisis. Don't you think it's the combination of—"

"I know exactly how my father felt now when he gave up his dreams of flying. How would that mean anything if you didn't have the right person to enjoy it with you," he told her. "I know how my mother felt when she gave up everything her father could give her." He smiled. "You haven't asked me to give up a thing."

The corner of her mouth tilted. "Yet," she said, letting a hint of her usual impulsiveness shine through.

"Yet," he said. "Can you give me a hint?"

"Old girlfriends," she said without hesitation.

"Done. Happily. Isn't that love? You were jealous of Christine?"

She was on the verge of admitting it. He only hoped he wasn't deluding himself now. But she sobered. "It was another part of the package," she said. "Of course I *thought* I was jealous. I was supposed to be your wife."

"You are my wife," he said pointedly.

"It was playacting," she said as if that explained everything. She shook her head. "That only goes to show you don't really know me. You only think you do."

"I know everything that's important."

She gave a frustrated sigh and tried to push him away. "Growing up, I was in trouble all the time. I'm impetuous and impulsive. I hop into one thing after another without thinking it through. Like this." She threw up her hands. He caught one of them and kissed it.

Shelby whispered shakily. "I've dreamed so long of a family of my own and babies I can love, that I started putting you in that role—"

He gently pressed his lips to hers, hushing her again. "Put me there, Shelby. When I said I didn't want a family, I was being flippant. I love my family."

"I know," she said softly.

The feeling expanding inside him felt far too big for his chest. "And I like kids."

"I know," she said again. "You were a teacher."

"I just couldn't picture anyone I'd want to have them with. All you have to promise is a little time to get readjusted to the idea," he added. The thought of sharing her with anyone was daunting. "The one thing you can't ask me to give up now is you," he said.

The sunshine smell of her hair filled his nose. He wanted her like he'd never wanted anything in his life.

"When I hold you," he said, drawing her completely into his arms, "I'm certain everything is right with the world. And," he added, "you make me smile." He traced her wide, wonderful mouth with one finger, hoping to coax it into the wide, wonderful smile. "Shelby Evans." He loved the way his name sounded with hers. He loved the way her head gradually fell back as if she was quietly savoring his hold on her. He loved the way she trembled in his arms.

"I love you," he said again slowly, making certain she didn't miss a word. "With every breath." That finally brought her arms hurtling around him as she pressed against his chest, close to his heart. "With every heartbeat." His arms closed tight. "With everything I am."

"Oh, Nick."

"So are you ever going to admit you love me?"

She shook her head helplessly. "I know I'm just

as delusional as you. And far too impulsive and..."
She looked up at him, her green eyes shimmering.
"But I love you, Nick Evans," she said passionately.

The kiss he tried to steal, she gave. And the I love
yous she had been so stingy with grazed his lips, his
cheek, his neck, his throat. She scattered them as if
they were stars in the sky...left them there...sprinkled
them with kisses. He finally took the words right out
of her mouth with another sweet taste of her lips.

"So when can we make this official," he finally
managed to draw away enough to ask.

"You don't consider what we have official," she
said, her smile glowing brighter with each word.

"It's legal, I suppose. But don't you want a real
wedding—"

"Our little wedding in Miami seemed real enough
to me." Her eyes gleamed. "Maybe it's time to move
on to the honeymoon."

The idea appealed to him. A lot. "Oh," he said,
"I forgot to tell you—I love your great ideas."

"Oh, Nick," she sighed. This time, she captured
his lips.

When his blood had boiled to the point of steam,
her fingers released one of the buttons on his shirt and
she tentatively slid her hand inside, next to his heart.

It soared.

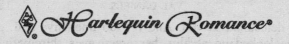

Get ready to meet the world's most eligible bachelors: they're sexy, successful and, best of all, they're all yours!

January 1998
Undercover Husband by Rebecca Winters (#3489)
Roman Lufka has been hired to protect Brittany Langford.
The easiest way to be by her side, twenty-four hours a
day, is to go undercover as Brittany's husband. But the
rough, tough P.I. finds himself facing his hardest
assignment yet—falling in love!

March 1998
Marriage on His Terms by Val Daniels (#3497)
Nick Evans needs a wife to secure an inheritance.
He doesn't need any kind of romantic involvement, so
he proposes marriage to the first woman he meets—
Shelby Wright. She's shocked, of course, but Nick can
be very persuasive.

*Bachelor Territory—There are two sides
to every story...and now it's his turn!*

Available wherever Harlequin books are sold.

shocking pink

THEY WERE ONLY WATCHING...

The mysterious lovers the three girls spied on were engaged in a deadly sexual game no one else was supposed to know about. Especially not Andie and her friends whose curiosity had deepened into a dangerous obsession....

Now fifteen years later, Andie is being watched by someone who won't let her forget the unsolved murder of "Mrs. X" or the sudden disappearance of "Mr. X." And Andie doesn't know who her friends are....

WHAT THEY SAW WAS MURDER.

ERICA SPINDLER

Available in February 1998 at your favorite retail outlet.

The Brightest Stars in Women's Fiction.™

Welcome to *Love Inspired*™

**A brand-new series of contemporary
inspirational love stories.**

Join men and women as they learn valuable lessons
about facing the challenges of today's world and
about life, love and faith.

**Look for the following March 1998
Love Inspired™ titles:**

CHILD OF HER HEART
by Irene Brand

A FATHER'S LOVE
by Cheryl Wolverton

WITH BABY IN MIND
by Arlene James

Available in retail outlets in February 1998.

LIFT YOUR SPIRITS AND GLADDEN YOUR HEART
with *Love Inspired!*™

Steeple
Hill™

LI398